BACK TO US

RACHEL HANNA

PROLOGUE

May, 1987

We stand there, backs facing the door leading from the garage into the house, pretending that nothing is going on in there. My sister, who is four years older than me, is clearly embarrassed in front of her newest boyfriend, Charlie.

I honestly don't know why she picks these ugly guys, but I won't go there. Needless to say, his thick dark hair cut into that sugar bowl look - complete with bangs - is not doing him any favors. And those bushy eyebrows are in need of help or possibly a hedge trimmer, but Lord knows I better not say anything. We sure aren't close as sisters. My opinions about her choice of boyfriends would be about as well-received as a kiss from a rabid porcupine.

So we stand there.

All of us.

My mother, trying to look strong but anxiously chewing on her nails and white-knuckling it not to light up a Virginia Slims cigarette, stands beside me. She's staring out of the open garage door, watching absolutely nothing. There's nothing to watch in this podunk little town anyway.

My sister is crossing her arms, like we're interfering with her schedule or something. Her hair has problems of its own with those big wing-like pieces on the sides, plastered on by industrial strength hairspray. And someone - I still don't remember who - gave her the ugliest blue eye shadow last Christmas, which she has caked on in an effort to woo Charlie, I suppose.

And then there's Charlie, who just looks like he wants to get out of here. I can't blame him. I do too.

The noises coming from inside the house are concerning. My Dad - typically the most mild-mannered man in America - is in there. I love him. I'm worried that he's getting hurt.

He's in there with my brother. My drug-addicted eighteen year old brother who's six-foot-three and strong as an ox. Actually, he's my half-brother, but we've been raised together so I don't normally think of him that way. Until recently. Until he started tearing the family apart.

We share a mother, and she married her first husband at sixteen, probably to escape a lot of her family life too. She got pregnant, had my brother, got divorced at seventeen and then married my and my sister's father.

And I thought things were going well. Until they weren't.

For awhile, I think they tried to hide the dysfunction from me. I'm twelve, but I'm not stupid. I'm what they refer to as "too smart for her own good".

Today, my brother has disrupted a family dinner. One of those Leave It To Beaver, sit around the kitchen table and pass the mashed potatoes kind of Sunday dinners. The kind that make your family look perfect, but don't reveal the cracks underneath.

Like your sweet, but severely alcoholic grandfather.

Or your also alcoholic uncle.

Or your crazy grandmother.

Or, in this case, your drug-fueled brother who is intent on hating the world and creating chaos wherever he goes.

It's the kind of life that either toughens you up or breaks you down, either makes you an addict yourself or makes you a tee-totaler who never wants to try a drug or rely on alcohol.

I want to be a tee-totaler.

"You will not act like this in our house!" I hear my father yelling. I hear things breaking. I know my father isn't doing it; he's "slow to anger", as my mother calls it. Easy going to the max.

But my brother isn't. Sounds like he's throwing a chair. Hope he doesn't hit my Dad with it.

I wonder why we're standing here, doing nothing. We're mostly women - except Charlie, as far as I know - so are we expected to just not get involved? Stand here and be safe?

Why aren't we calling the police? For one thing, the phone is on the wall of the kitchen and going back in there right now is not an option. For another thing, my mother wants to keep up appearances. The last thing she wants is for the neighbors to know our dirty little secret - that we have a "druggy" in the house and he's destroying our family.

My brother - oh, his name is Danny, by the way - changed almost overnight. Obviously, my family has addiction prone DNA or something, so when he tried his first bit of weed or pot or whatever you call it - well, he liked it. A lot. Too much.

And that led to other stuff, I guess. My Mom tries to shield me from most of that. She tries to make out like everything is okay. Our family is normal. All families have stuff like this going on.

The only problem is I'm not sure I believe her.

I can't tell anyone about this. It's a secret. Which is why we're in the garage, so Charlie doesn't see it.

Do they think Charlie is stupid? Maybe deaf? I see ears poking out from under his awful haircut, so I'm assuming they work.

I think a passing cat would know what is going on inside of our house right now.

And then there's silence, followed by a loud door slam and my brother running out the front door. He jumps into his new Trans

3

Am, a gift from our grandparents who give him everything he wants no matter how bad he screws up, and speeds off.

And then we go back inside, lock the doors and continue eating Sunday dinner like nothing happened. Except we have one less chair at the dinner table - because it's smashed into a million pieces on the other side of the living room.

CHAPTER 1

P *resent Day*

It's funny the things that you remember when you come back to the place that made you into who you are. Like a time machine, I feel immediately transported to the twelve year old little girl who lived in this house. This small, brick ranch in a quiet neighborhood.

I stand in front of it, thankful that it's on the market for sale so the owners don't think I'm a stalker. I'm also thankful the agent opened it for me, so I could take a look inside, take a walk down memory lane.

Of course, it helped that I told a little fib about maybe wanting to make an offer on it. But I have no intentions of doing that. Visiting the memories is one thing; living with them again is quite another.

I walk up to the front door and immediately have my first memory of all of the Easter pictures taken on the front steps. Some with my parents together; some with just me and my Mom and sister.

Before and after a family split apart.

I enter the foyer first. It's smaller than I remember. I

recall the closet where my mother kept the sex education book she tried to use to teach us the birds and the bees. It brings a smile to my face as I think about how embarrassed she was trying to explain everything to me with that inadequate children's book that had questionable illustrations.

Thankfully, I said I wasn't interested, and she was more than happy to toss it back up into the dark depths of the little closet. I never saw it again and learned about sex like every other kid - in a public school classroom.

The house looks different. Brighter, updated, but still so familiar. And so much smaller now that I am so much bigger.

I go into the den, where we watched TV and hung out with guests when I was growing up. I remember the huge console TV we had and the brown shag carpeting that was eventually replaced with plush white carpeting when that came into fashion. The dark wood paneling has now been painted a brighter cream colored shade, although it still feels a bit rough against my hand as I run my fingers across a section of it.

I remember sitting in this room in 1986, home sick from school, and watching the Challenger space shuttle blow up before my very eyes on TV. It was one of the first shocking things I'd ever seen, and I often thought about that shattering of the pieces in mid air as being similar to the feeling one gets when their family falls apart before their very eyes. Everything is going along so well, and then it just isn't. There's no warning, only destruction.

"Ms. Sanders?" the agent - whose name I think is Eileen - says from behind me as I stand motionless in the living room.

"Yes?" I ask, turning around and noticing her repeatedly checking her phone, ostensibly for the current time.

"I'm really sorry, but my son has missed his bus, and I've got to run over to the school to pick him up…"

"Oh sure. I understand."

"Can you wait out there on the porch for a bit? I'll be right back."

She's trying to save her commission, which I totally understand. Even though I'm not in the market to buy. I'm just here for a few days, walking down memory lane. Which currently feels like walking on broken glass.

"Take your time. I think I'll just walk around the property for a bit, if that's okay?"

"Oh, yes! That's not a problem at all," the perky agent says. I watch her immovable blond bob, wondering what kind of hairspray she uses that keeps it from swaying in the gentle Georgia breeze. It's early fall, and I notice the leaves changing to a deep shade of gold on the big oak tree out front. "The owners are out of town, so walk around and take a look at whatever you want. I'll be back in a flash!"

It occurs to me that she might need a medication to even out her peppy mood, but maybe that's just the psychologist in me. Thankfully, I can't prescribe medication.

I first take a seat on the brick steps in front of the home, the place where I sat for hours as a kid, usually listening to the large boom box teetering on my lap. I close my eyes and suck in a deep breath of air, the smell of burning leaves in the distance reminding me of what Georgia is like in those autumn months before the unpredictable winter sets in.

The tiny town of Peach Valley sits in the foothills of the north Georgia mountains, shaded by the alternating light grays and dark blues of the mountains towering above.

For much of my life, Peach Valley offered an idyllic childhood with the Pumpkin Parade in the fall and the 4th of July parade in the heat of summer. Back then, a kid could walk miles to the local drug store to purchase copious amounts of rock candy without worrying about being snatched by some child predator. In fact, I spent many a summer walking to the local shopping center parking lot - at least a mile away - to ride the ferris wheel at the traveling carnival that came to town a few times each year.

Those were different times.

There was no social media. Bullying was expected and something we all had to overcome. Kids played outside until the street lights came on, and their parents rang dinner bells to signal supper time. Lightning bugs were something to chase, and cartwheels were something to be perfected in the itchy grass of every kid's front yard.

There were no cell phones, only phones hanging on the wall with rotary dials and curly cords. There were no reality shows, only three channels plus PBS. I smile as I think about the aluminum foil contraption that we kept on the rabbit ears above the TV just so we could watch Family Ties and Growing Pains.

I look over at the big oak tree and remember the one time I rode a motorcycle in my whole life, and my brother ran us both into that tree. As I walk toward it, I can still see the huge gouge out of the trunk, and I am reminded that people can have tough things happen to them, but still rise up stronger even with deep scars. I can't help but smile thinking back to that moment, though. Although I was so angry at my brother at the time, it was one of the only times that I can remember us doing something that was a brother/sister thing. Before he turned to drugs. Before he made a string of bad decisions that destroyed any hope for a relationship with me.

As I stand looking at the oak tree, my eyes move to the left toward the street in front of my old home, and a wave of other memories sweep across my consciousness. The house - about the same size as ours - sits diagonally. It's a tan color now, but back then it was dark gray with equally dark shutters. A cast of rental families had moved in and out of that house for years, as if a revolving door brought them in and then ushered them out months later.

But one family springs to mind, and a small smile claims ownership of my mouth for a moment as I allow myself to think back to that early summer day.

Late May, 1987

It's already so freaking hot. I really wish my mother would listen to my constant pleadings to move to a beach somewhere. After all, I've only been to the beach twice in my life, neither time I can even recall. At least the heat would be bearable at the beach.

Being the third child can really suck sometimes. My parents seemed to have a lot more money when my brother and sister were younger, which I guess makes sense because it was one less mouth to feed. So they had all of these grand adventures - evidence of which I can see on those God-awful reel-to-reel family slideshows they force us to watch at least once a year - well before I was born.

They had all the cool stuff - an above ground pool, a bigger house, even a station wagon! By the time I came along, we were living in a smaller house with my Dad's work van and another car that definitely wasn't the cool station wagon I craved. I learned a long time ago not to complain or ask why we didn't take more vacations or have a bigger house like some of my other friends. I got the message loud and clear to be thankful for what I have and stop complaining.

So today I am walking to my friend's house, as I do almost every day. I saw a new family move into the rental house the other day. Actually, I saw a woman and what appeared to be a little girl. I can see everything out of my bedroom window, although none of it seems particularly exciting.

I make it to Tabitha's house, but she isn't home. I kind of want to jump on her trampoline, but I also don't want to do it alone, so I head back toward my house trying to think of a way to break the boredom.

I feel like an only child even though I have a brother and a

9

sister. My sister is into hanging out with her friends and dating ugly boys. My brother is into drugs and dating sluts. So, yeah, I'm feeling lonelier by the day. All of my friends seem to have good relationships with their siblings. They have these cool, built-in friendships that I just don't have.

As I walk across the main road that runs just behind my house, I notice the late spring yellow pollen sitting in puddles on the sides of the road, floating on top of the little pools of recent rainwater. Normally, the pollen is long gone by now, but for some reason it hung around this year - probably to further aggravate my allergies and asthma.

I feel bad because my mother installed an attic fan in our house the summer before I was diagnosed with asthma. It wasn't until she turned it on and started sucking the outside inside of our house that we realized I am highly allergic to most of the things floating in the Georgia air. So now the attic fan is an ugly reminder of my irritable lungs and the wasted money she spent. Maybe that's why we can't go to the beach. The attic fan sucked up all of our money.

As I enter the small neighborhood where we live, I get a wisp of pollen straight into my nasal passages just as I pass the ugly gray rental house that is diagonal to my own home.

"Achoo!" A huge sneeze escapes me, causing me to stop for a moment and bend over from the force.

"Bless you."

Great. Now I'm hearing voices that aren't there. I look around, but I see no one.

"Achoo!" I let out again. I'm one of those "multiple sneezers" who cannot just sneeze one time.

"Bless you."

I look around again, scanning my field of vision and seeing nothing. The old, mean man next door to my house isn't outside. The alcoholic rose gardening man next to the rental house is usually still nursing a hangover at this time of day. And no one is outside at the rental house.

And because they come in threes...

"Achoo!"

"Bless you."

"Okay, where are you?" I yell out, probably looking like a lunatic standing in the middle of the street as I throw my arms up in the air.

Then I hear a chuckle. Deep, as in male, but not deep enough to be a man.

"Over here," he says. I turn toward the rental house and finally see him, his silhouette dark behind the screen of one of the front windows. "I'm Dawson."

I walk closer, wondering why he doesn't just come outside and speak to me like a normal person. Besides, I'm wondering if he's cute because that would be fantastic gossip to share with Tabitha later.

"Indy," I say, telling him the shortened version of my name. As I walk closer to his window, I can see most of his face now. He's smiling, and it's a nice smile.

"Indy? Like Indiana? Or Indianapolis? One of my step dads liked racing..." He's leaning on the windowsill, his tanned skin standing out to me first. I'm so white that there isn't even a crayon color that would match my skin, so I envy tan people.

"No. Like Indigo."

"Indigo?"

"It's the shade of color between blue and violet."

He cocks his head at me and smiles. "That's weird."

"Tell my parents. They say it matches the unique color of my eyes," I say dramatically as I lean against his window.

He leans in, almost pressing his face to the screen and stares at me. "Hm. Nice."

"What?" I can feel my face starting to flush, another reason to hate pale skin.

"Nothing."

"So, you're new here..." I say, trying to change the subject.

11

Where is Tabitha when I need her? She always knows how to move a conversation right along.

"Yeah. We just moved in a couple of days ago."

"What do your mom and dad do?" *I'm not sure why I'm asking. Making small talk sucks.*

He clears his throat. "My mom works at the cafe on Maplewood. And she just left my latest dad," he says, using air quotes around the last word.

I pluck a stray, dead leaf from between the bricks outlining his window and nervously break it apart with my fingers. "Latest dad?" *My parents have always told me I ask too many questions, but my curiosity is getting the best of me.*

"Yep. He was number four, if you don't include my real dad."

"Where is he?"

"Who knows? Left when I was a baby. I don't remember him at all, but I'm told that I have his stubborn streak and his ability to lie easily, so that's nice..." *I like his sarcasm, and for a moment I wonder if he might be lying to me.*

"Well, I better get home. Almost dinner time."

"Yeah," he says as I start walking away. "Will you be dancing tonight?"

I stop dead in my tracks. "Excuse me?" *I say, turning around dramatically.*

"I like to watch you dance. It's funny."

Oh. My. God. He's been watching me dance in my room at night. Nothing raunchy. I'm not even thirteen years old yet. But my Mom bought me this cool strobe light for my last birthday, and I create my own dance party in my room at night. I can't wait until I'm old enough to go to one of those cool dance clubs with my friends.

Every night, while my Dad is still working and my mother is smoking cigarettes on the back patio, I dance. Up until now, I thought no one could see me. After all, the rental house had been empty for months and the old people next door go to sleep early and seem to be somewhat deaf.

"Do you know how creepy that is? For you to watch me?"

"Do you know how impossible it is to ignore when your neighbor's window is open and it looks like a lightning storm in there?"

I purse my lips for a moment before huffing and turning around. But I can't stop myself from smiling as I walk home.

WHEN THE AGENT finally returns to finish showing me the house, I'm filled with a mixture of longing to relive some of my childhood memories and running as far from Peach Valley as I can get.

Yes, there were good memories. But there were some bad ones too. I tell my counseling clients that those tough times turn us into warriors. They give us stories that we can use to help others who are one step behind us.

Right now, it all feels so trite. Too easy. Not nearly complicated enough.

"And this is the kitchen, of course," the agent says. What did she think I thought it was? Did I appear to be confused about what an oven and refrigerator do? "The previous owner upgraded the appliances about three years ago…" Her words are going over my head as I look around the room.

There's the place where our kitchen table sat and we ate dinners as a complete family. And then *not* as a complete family.

There's the phone jack on the wall where I chatted with my girlfriends and where I answered the phone when my father called to say he wasn't coming home anymore. That my mother wanted a divorce. That my siblings were the only ones who got the complete family package, and I got the broken home downgrade.

Looking back now, as an adult, I understand. But as a child I didn't. My parents seemed happy. I loved my father like every girl should. But it just didn't work for them.

Even now, when I counsel a married couple looking at divorce, I want to plead with them to keep it together. But I know that isn't logical or even a good plan if they have kids. But the kid in me - the 12-year old little girl whose world was rocked just after August that year - wants to tell them that divorce changes the lives of everyone involved.

The separate birthday parties.

The separate Christmases.

The weekend drop offs and pickups.

"Did you have any questions about the kitchen?" she asks.

"No. I think I've seen everything I need to see in here. Do you mind if I take a quick walk around the backyard?"

"Of course. Take your time. I just need to make a quick phone call," she says.

I walk back into the living room and turn right to go out the door onto the covered patio. I stop for a moment to remember when my father and his friend put that metal roof over the small concrete patio.

The yard looks much the same, boxy and plain with a chain link fence around it. But it's not the grass I'm looking at. It's the place between two large oak trees where the wooden swing sat. There's a metal one there now, with one of those fancy cloth awnings covering it. It's just not the same.

Still, I walk over there as if drawn by some magnetic field, and sit down. As I start to swing, I close my eyes, blocking out the sound of the cars behind my old house, and I summon back memories that should be long forgotten.

June 1987

"So did you see me dancing last night?" I ask Dawson, as I do almost everyday that we hang out.

"Of course I did. You called me, remember?"

That's our thing. I play my songs and dance with my strobe light, and he listens to the music from the other end of the phone while watching me. I've invited him over a million times, but his mother is a strange mixture of not trusting anyone and bringing random men home to live with her young son and daughter.

We sit at the edge of the creek behind our neighborhood, a favorite place to look for tadpoles and eat muscadine berries.

"I think my mom is going to get married again soon," he says softly.

"Why do you think that? Didn't she just get a divorce from that Larry guy?"

"Yeah," he says, skipping a rock across the short expanse of water. "I'm never getting married."

"I'm definitely getting married."

He laughs, but it's not the laugh of someone who heard something funny. It's a sad laugh. "Adults never stay together forever. That's a fairy tale. I heard Larry say that to my mother when she threw his clothes out on the lawn of our old house after he cheated with the neighbor lady."

"I don't believe that. My parents have been married over twenty years, so Larry was wrong. True love lasts forever, but you have to find your one true love. Nobody else will do."

"Maybe so, but I'm still not getting married."

"Okay! No one's asking you!" I say with a force that surprises even me.

Dawson looks at me, wide-eyed. "What's wrong with you?"

"Nothing," I say. Maybe I like him more than I thought I did.

THE AGENT WALKS TOWARD ME. "Ms. Sanders? Are you alright?"

I stand up quickly, almost losing my balance in the process. "Yes. Why do you ask?"

"Because you've been sitting out here... sort of staring... for about half an hour..."

My face flushes with embarrassment. "I'm so sorry, Eileen. I guess time got away from me."

She smiles. "Should I assume you have fallen so in love that you want to make an offer on this place?"

I force a smile in return. "I'll certainly give it some thought. How about I call you tomorrow?"

Her smile fades, and she nods before I follow her back into the house and out the front door.

CHAPTER 2

A lot has changed about Peach Valley, but much has also stayed the same. The old town area still looks like it did when I was a kid, complete with the old drug store and bookstore. I walk past it, peering into the big window out front, wondering if it still smells of mold and old books. I also wonder how it has survived the invention of ebook readers and the proliferation of giant, impersonal bookstores.

I make my way down the sidewalk with big sunglasses covering my face, hoping that no one recognizes me. I haven't been back here in many years; not since I moved my mother to the assisted living center when she got early onset dementia so many years ago. Even then, I rarely came home after leaving for college.

But now I have no choice.

I glance up and finally see the whole reason I'm here. Although I'm an unwilling participant in this thing, one can't ignore legal documents.

"Evans, Clarke and Peenee," the woman behind the desk

says into the phone in a thick Southern accent. First, I want to bust out laughing at the last name "Peenee", but then I imagine what the man behind that name went through growing up with that kind of name. She waves at me to sit down as she finishes up the call.

I find a seat in the small, old waiting area. It looks like time stood still 'round about 1975 in this place, the cheap wood paneling still adorning the walls. Being an attorney's office, I'd expected a little nicer place, but this is Peach Valley after all. Being in Charleston for so many years has spoiled me on historic buildings and beautiful features.

"Can I help you, hon?" the woman asks.

I stand back up. "I'm here to see Ethan Clarke. He'll be expecting me."

Ethan went to high school with me and took over the family legal business when his father retired. I haven't seen him since graduation day, so I was surprised to get the call from him a few days ago that he needed to see me ASAP about an urgent legal matter. I offered to pay for his trip up to Charleston, but he declined saying that he needed me to come "home".

My mother's estate - what little it was - was settled months ago, so I have no idea what he wants with me. Maybe she had an old bank account or insurance policy I don't know about, but Ethan wouldn't tell me anything over the phone. Small town folk can be odd that way.

"Mr. Clarke will see you now," the woman says, and I instantly smile at the thought of calling Ethan "mister" anything. I follow her through the ugly brown door and down a small hallway that leads to Ethan's office. He's smiling before I even make it past the entryway.

"Well, I'll be! Indy Stone in the flesh," he says, walking around his desk and hugging me tightly. I stiffen for a moment and then return the hug.

"Sanders, actually," I say, correcting him.

"Didn't you get divorced?" he asks, pointing to a fake leather covered chair with big metal rivets attaching it to the thick wood frame. I take a seat and place my purse in my lap, almost like a shield from the question.

"Yes, but I kept my married name," I say. I don't know why I kept it. One would think getting rid of the husband would mean getting rid of the last name. But as a fairly popular therapist in Charleston, I didn't want to lose my branding.

"Hm. I always thought Indy Stone sounded like a superhero. If you decide to change it back, let me know. I can handle the paperwork," he says with a wink. I notice he's a grown man now with pearly white teeth and thinning hair - a far cry from the star of the football team he once was. There's a gold band on his left hand, and pictures of a blond woman and three adorable kids on his desk. Ethan is a grown up. It's weird.

"Ethan, why am I here? I had to change my whole schedule around for my counseling clients, so I hope there's a really good reason for all the mystery."

"Indy, your brother passed away a few weeks ago."

I feel the air leave my lungs, but I'll be damned if I'm going to let it show on my face. I let go of my brother years ago when it became apparent that he would never change; he'd always be the self-centered person he had been since the day I was born... and probably before.

Danny was five years older than me, and his drug problems tore our family apart all those years ago. My parents divorced, my mother battled ulcers for years and he never seemed to take any responsibility for it. The moment I hit adulthood and could make the decision, I cut him from my life. Slowly, the whole family did.

First it was Amy, but she had basically cut me out too.

19

That sisterly bond just wasn't there. When she moved across the country and got married, that pretty much sealed our fate.

And then my father cut him out, but that was easy since he wasn't blood related anyway. Although he'd adopted my brother so many years before, the drug addiction and rage issues my brother had destroyed the possibility of a reconciliation.

And then there was my mother. She took the longest, but she finally realized that she couldn't save him. Her life had been put on hold for so many years, through his multiple rehab attempts and stints in jail. She finally gave up. And then shortly afterward, her memory started to fade. Sometimes I think that might have been a godsend for her because who wants to remember the son that let them down?

There were a few times I tried to mend fences, tried to accept him for who he was, tried to be his sister. Every single time, he showed me his true colors. He'd constantly been in trouble with the law, and when he needed money he came calling. Finally, I decided to save myself and I cut all ties. Honestly, it had been a very relaxing decade or so since his last contact with me, and that made me feel very guilty to even think.

This basically made me an only child.

When I fell for my brother's sob story the last time, he took me for thousands of dollars, and I decided to let that part of my life go. I excised my brother from my heart and put the idea of him in a tiny mental box that I never opened.

Until today.

"Okay… And what does that have to do with me? I'm sure you know we had no relationship, Ethan. If this is about some bill he owes…"

"It's not about bills, Indy," he says, taking a deep breath before continuing. "It's about his daughter."

I stare at him like he's speaking another language. And now I hear a roaring sound inside my head that I assume to be blood pumping way too hard around my body.

"Daughter? What daughter?"

Ethan sucks both of his lips in then smiles at me sympathetically. "Your brother had a ten-year old daughter, Indy. Her name is Harper."

"I can't believe this…" I stammer, unsure of what to say.

"And he named you as her guardian."

He says it softly and quickly, as if that will keep me from noticing the weight of the words he just uttered.

"What? Where is her mother?"

"Her mother died of a drug overdose right after she was born. Your brother cleaned up his act, Indy. He had a job and built a life for himself and Harper. But then there was an accident at work…"

I can't hear him now. What kind of person just randomly leaves their kid to someone they don't even really know? He hasn't known me since I was a teenager myself, and even then he was so stoned he probably wouldn't have known me if I'd passed him on the street.

Yet a part of me grieves. He *was* my brother. There had been good times. A part of me loves him, and I am very angry at that part of myself right now. It's a strange feeling really. I grieved the relationship with him - and what I wanted him to be as my brother - long ago.

But now I grieve for the loss of hope that we can ever be real siblings. I grieve over the knowledge that there will never be a day that I can say, "This is my brother Danny. We had a rough road, but we're closer now than we've ever been because he cared enough to get clean for his little sister." Somewhere, deep down, in the recesses of my heart and mind, I've apparently been hoping and dreaming that all things could be made right.

"Ethan, I can't do this. I have a life in Charleston. I'm not equipped to take care of a ten-year old kid, and certainly not one that belonged to my brother."

He looks at me as if he can't believe what I'm saying, yet doesn't judge me.

"She's had a tough time, Indy. Harper has been with her father for her whole life, and he had some issues here and there. But he's all she ever knew. She's been stuck in a foster home since he died…"

"Don't you do that! Don't you guilt trip me, Ethan Clarke!" I say, standing up and being a lot louder than is appropriate in the small office.

"I'm not trying to guilt you. I'm being honest with you."

"There has to be someone else."

"There's no one else, Indy. Trust me. I've scoured both family trees, and you're it. If you don't take Harper, she will get lost in a system that is already overflowing with kids who need homes."

"What about Amy?" I say, knowing full well that my sister would never take on a task like this.

"It's Amy. You know better than that. Besides, she lives in Seattle with Ben and her own three kids."

Kids I've only seen on Skype and the occasional Facebook post. Yeah, we just aren't all that close.

He stands and walks to where I'm staring out the window, watching people mill about in front of the sandwich shop.

"Look, Indy, I know this is hard. Danny was not an easy guy. I remember."

"How did you know?" I ask softly, thinking that our family did a pretty good job of hiding our skeletons.

"My uncle was a cop. He arrested Danny several times."

"Lovely."

"And the truth is, if Harper ends up as a foster kid, the

chances that she'll ever have a family are slim. She'll likely just be sent from foster home to foster home, and who knows what could happen to her. I'm just being honest, Indy. Maybe this is your chance to change someone's life."

I like to think I change lives everyday, with every counseling session. But in reality I don't. I just let people talk about their problems. I nod along. I give ideas on what they can try. But taking in an orphan, well that's a whole other level of changing lives.

"I need some time," I say, because it really seems like the only thing I can say.

"There's one other thing." Again, he's speaking fast so I don't flip out.

"What?"

He walks back behind his desk and retrieves a paper. "Danny stipulated that he wanted Harper to stay in Peach Valley so she could finish school here. He wrote this will a couple of years ago right after Harper made the honor roll…"

"You can't be serious, Ethan. My whole business and life is in Charleston. I cannot… I will not… move back to Peach Valley."

"Even if that's what's best for Harper?" he asks.

"How do we know that? The schools where I live are top notch. Peach Valley is a small town with no opportunities…"

"Indy, come on. Surely you've noticed that Peach Valley isn't the same as it was twenty years ago?"

To me, it seems exactly the same which feels like a blessing and a curse.

I sigh. "I need some time, Ethan. This is all a little… much."

I stand and start walking toward the door. "When would you like to meet your niece?" he asks.

"I'll call you," I say before shutting the door behind me.

~

"Are you sure your mother isn't going to get mad?" I ask as we walk down the mile stretch of road toward the shopping center.

"If she found out, then yeah," he says, kicking a rock in front of his beat up white Reebok hightops. We've spent practically every day together since we met. It's nice to have a new friend who lives so close to me.

The plan today is to walk to the store, buy as much rock candy as we can eat and play games at the traveling carnival that's in town. Dawson's mother told him to stay home, so if she finds out he went to the store, she's going to get mad.

"But won't she see us walking down the street?"

"Nope. She's probably making out with her new boyfriend at his apartment."

The thought gives me the heebie jeebies. "But it's going to be dinnertime soon. Won't she need to come home and cook you dinner?"

He sighs. "My mom doesn't cook, Indy. She's barely a mother."

I feel an unfamiliar pang in my chest where my health teacher told me my heart was located. My mom cooks me dinner. We always have a full meal every night. Why doesn't Dawson's mom do that, I wonder.

"So what will you eat tonight?"

"Probably peanut butter and jelly. Or maybe a can of ravioli if I can find one. I love ravioli."

We're having fried chicken with mashed potatoes and green beans tonight. And homemade biscuits. But Dawson might not even get ravioli? He's a twelve year old boy who needs to eat, or at least that's what my mother would say.

"You wanna eat dinner at my house?"

"Nah. I'd get in trouble for that."

24

We keep walking for awhile without talking. "Do you like having so many different dads?"

I know it's a dumb question, but I'm really wondering. Maybe he gets to have Christmases and birthdays with a huge extended family. At least I hope so.

"No. Some of them aren't very nice people."

"What did they do?"

He stops and stares at his shoes for a moment. "If I show you something, do you promise not to tell anyone?" I nod.

My heart clenches again as he takes my hand and pulls me toward the woods, out of the view of passing cars. Without a word, he pulls up the back of his t-shirt and shows me a long scar that stretches from one side of his back to the other.

I reach out and touch it, and he jumps a little at my touch but allows me to run my index finger across the length of it. It's still pink and not at all like the scar on my knee from three years ago when I fell off my bike. It's raised and still has this angry redness around it.

"Does it hurt?" I ask as he pulls his shirt back down.

"Not as much anymore," he looks down at his feet.

"Who did that, Dawson?" I feel something brewing deep inside of me, like angry butterflies in my stomach.

"The last step dad. Apparently, I didn't say thank you to my mother fast enough after she cooked me dinner for once." He leans against a tree, resting his lower back and crossing his arms. He's my age, but he looks so much older than his years.

I have no idea what to say. I've never even gotten a spanking. "What did he hit you with?"

"A belt." I wait for him to elaborate, but he doesn't. And I don't think I want to know anymore.

"You didn't deserve that, Dawson. No one does."

He finally looks at me, and I swear tears are welling up in his big brown eyes. I always want to cry when I see someone else about *to cry, and I definitely don't want him to see my ugly cry. My sister says I look like a rabid walrus when I cry. She's so nice.*

"I used to think I couldn't trust anyone," he says softly.

"Used to?"

"Yeah." He looks back up at me, and the smallest of smiles appears on his face. "Until I met you."

I return his smile, and feel my heart skip a beat for the first time, like in one of those Harlequin romance novels my mom tries to hide under her mattress.

"Race you the rest of the way?" I say, talking big since my asthma would stop me in about twenty feet.

"Nah. Let's just walk," he says, taking my hand and walking back up to the road. As we walk to the store, he never lets go of my hand, and for some reason I don't want him to.

I SIT on the porch of my old house, hoping the neighbors don't call the police on me. I shouldn't be here again. I don't know what draws me here.

I do have some fond memories of my home. Big Christmas dinners. Easter egg hunts in the backyard. The huge fig tree that almost covered our entire front yard. Even after my father cut it to the ground and burned the stump, the thing grew back twice as big. It was even on the front page of the local newspaper once.

"Indy? Is that you?" I hear a female voice say from the street. I look up and see someone who looks familiar, but I can't remember her name or how I know her.

"Hi. Yes, I'm Indy."

The woman laughs. "Did you buy your old house back?"

I look at the real estate sign still standing in the yard. "Oh. No. I'm just… reminiscing." I walk toward her when I realize she isn't going away and she meets me in the middle of the driveway.

She's definitely older than me, and her face looks so familiar. "You may not remember me. I'm Lisa, Agnes Watkins' daughter."

Then it hits me. She's the oldest daughter of our neighbors from across the street. She was a few years ahead of me in school, so I'm surprised she remembers me.

"Oh yes, Lisa. I remember you! You drove that cool little red sports car, right?" For some reason, that memory makes me smile. I remember watching her zip up and down the streets, and I think I also remember my brother flirting with her.

"Yes, that was a good car."

"So, you still live in the neighborhood?" I ask, surprise evident in my voice. She cocks her head and smiles.

"Of course. Why would I leave?" It occurs to me that she's just as surprised that anyone would choose to leave Peach Valley as I am that anyone would willingly stay there forever.

"Right. How's your mother?"

"Oh, honey, she passed away almost ten years ago now." I feel a weird loss, like I should have known. Agnes was a kind woman, and she baked the best oatmeal raisin cookies on the planet. Every Halloween, she made brownies with extra fudge baked into them, and there was a line on her front stoop as we all waited our turn to get one dropped into our buckets and bags.

"I'm so sorry for your loss."

"And I was so sorry to hear about Danny. Terrible accident, I heard."

"Yes. Terrible." I don't know what to say. I didn't even ask Ethan what kind of accident it was because what does it matter? He's gone, and I'm left with an impossible situation.

"His little girl is just a peach. Spitting image of her Daddy, isn't she?"

I swallow hard and bite my lip. "I wouldn't know, Lisa. I've never met her."

Again, she looks confused and her eyebrows knit together like someone is pulling strings behind her head. "You've never met your niece?"

"No. To be honest, Danny and I hadn't spoken in many years. We had a lot of... history. Actually, I just found out that he even had a daughter."

She smiles sympathetically, but I can feel her judgment. The problem with keeping family secrets is that decisions based on those secrets look very selfish in the end. I look like the world's worst sister, but I have my reasons for breaking ties with my brother. Sometimes, you have to save yourself.

"Well, I don't want to pry about that, but let me tell you that Harper is just a delight. A sweet, sweet girl. Fiery, to be sure. But smart as a whip."

"How do you know Harper?"

"She was in my class last year. I'm a teacher over at the elementary school now." The pride on her face is apparent.

"Oh. Well, good for you. I mean, teaching the kids and all," I say, suddenly sounding like a babbling idiot. "So she's a good kid?"

I don't know why visions of a miniature version of my brother are invading my head. Thoughts of going through what my mother went through with him are all I can think about. The rehabs. The arguments. The calls from police. The irony of a siren in the distance breaks my chain of memories.

"Yes, she is. I haven't seen her since Danny... well, you know. But I hear she's struggling, Indy. They were very close."

I feel like a knife is digging into my heart. Above all else,

I'm a human being. I'm a freaking therapist. I can't leave this kid - part of my brother or not - hanging out in the wind.

"Listen, I hate to cut this short, Lisa, but I have a phone call to make. Do you mind if we chat later?"

She nods and smiles before returning to her afternoon walk as I sit back down on the front steps, pulling my cell phone from my pocket.

"Hi, Eileen. This is Indigo Sanders. You showed the house on Oakdale... I think I'd like to make an offer."

CHAPTER 3

I can't recall ever feeling so nervous. Closing on my old house had been tough, knowing that I was buying back all of the memories I had there, good and bad. But getting ready to meet my niece - my new daughter - is even tougher.

ETHAN HANDLED all of the paperwork days ago, but I wanted to have the house ready for her. The small three bedroom house will be plenty for us. I claimed the master bedroom with its own tiny bathroom, and I'm putting Harper in my sister's old room. My old bedroom will be my office, mainly because it feels much like a shrine and I just can't give it up to anyone else.

I FOUND the decision to leave my life in Charleston behind to be easier than I thought it would. Sure, the news Ethan delivered about having a niece who was now my responsibility had rocked me to the core at first. But then something else took over. Protectiveness. She's my family, and I can't leave her to the wolves. Sometimes, you have to make decisions based on what's right and not what you want to do.

THE LAST FEW days have also been full of calling clients in Charleston and explaining that I'm not coming back, at least not for the foreseeable future. Most understood, but some were upset. I helped them connect with other therapists that I trust, hoping that my life change doesn't throw their lives off the rails. I also called my friend, Pam, who is a real estate agent in Charleston to handle the renting of my current home on the water.

I'LL MISS THAT PLACE. It was an oasis after listening to everyone's problems all day. And now, here I stand in the house that both built me and broke me down.

BUT NOW I'M just waiting. Nothing between me and sudden parenthood. I stand at the window of my old bedroom and stare at the rental house where Dawson lived all those years ago, and memories flood me yet again.

JULY 1987

I HAVEN'T HEARD from Dawson today. Normally, I hear from him by now, but I don't think he's come outside at all.

WE'VE GROWN a lot closer since he showed me his scar. He tells me all the time that he can trust me, and it feels good to know that he does. I've never had a friend like him, not even Tabitha, and I know we'll be friends forever.

OR MAYBE WE'LL even get married someday.

NAH, Dawson says he'll never get married. I guess maybe it's because his mother has ruined that for him. Sometimes I try to imagine what it's like to have divorced parents and then all of these new dads coming in and out. I just can't imagine.

"INDY, I'm going to the store," my mother says through my closed door.

"OKAY. What time is Dad getting home?" I call back. There's a weird pause before she answers, and then her voice is flat.

"I DON'T KNOW."

I WATCH her leave out the window, and then I decide to go investigate where Dawson is. I'm worried about him. His mother's new boyfriend has been coming to the house a lot lately, and I don't like the looks of that man. He's scraggly, as my mother would call it.

I THROW on my Michael Jackson Thriller t-shirt and neon pink high top sneakers before heading outside, locking the front door behind me. Dawson and I are both obsessed with Michael Jackson. I think I've almost mastered the moonwalk, but Dawson just laughs at me every time I try to do it.

As I GET *close to his house, suddenly fire trucks run screaming to his driveway. Several firemen jump out and go to the door, and I start backing up, watching from a safe distance. I have no idea what's going on, but my heart is pounding against my rib cage like a jackhammer.*

AFTER A FEW MINUTES OF LOUD, *inaudible talking inside the house, the firemen come out, get into their truck and drive away. How weird. I decide to risk his mother getting mad at my immediate arrival and knock on the door.*

WHEN SHE SWINGS *the door open, she's pursing her lips and her face is red with anger. I can see Dawson sitting on the tiny floral love seat in his living room with his head in his hands.*

"WHAT DO YOU WANT?" *she asks.*

"I... UM... SAW THE FIRETRUCKS..."

"YES, *my genius son thought it would be funny to prank call the fire department!" she yells over her shoulder.*

DAWSON LOOKS *up and shakes his head. "I didn't do it, Mama. I* swear!" Tears are running down his face, and it makes me sad. I've never seen Dawson cry before.

"Don't you lie to me, Dawson!" she says. For some reason, she opens the door and allows me inside. I sit down next to Dawson, hoping my presence gives him some kind of support.

"Dawson, did you do that?" I whisper. He looks at me with pain in his eyes.

"Of course not, Indy."

"You're not leaving this house until you tell the truth," his mother says, walking into the kitchen. She's slamming pots and pans around so loudly that I can barely talk to him. I see her pull a bottle from behind one of the canisters on the kitchen counter and take a long sip of the amber colored liquid before putting it back in its hiding place.

"You promise? You didn't do that? Because it would be horrible if you did. The fire department has real emergencies to deal with..."

He looks at me pleadingly. "I didn't do it, Indy. Why don't you believe me?"

"Well, why did they show up then?" I whisper.

. . .

"I HAVE NO IDEA." He hangs his head again. Maybe someone prank called and gave his address. Maybe they misunderstood someone's address. I have no idea how these things work.

I WALK to the kitchen where his mother is bracing herself against the counter and hanging her head. I summon every ounce of courage in my body. "Ma'am, with all due respect, I don't think Dawson did this. He's a good kid, and he would never lie to me."

SHE TURNS and looks at me. "You don't know how my son really is. He lies. He's been lying since he knew how to talk. He lies just like his worthless father did." Images of the scar across his back flash through my mind. He sure didn't lie about that.

I TURN to see that Dawson isn't on the sofa anymore. He went to his room, apparently, and his mother walks out of the kitchen and down the hall. I don't know what to do with myself, so I just sit back down on the sofa.

A FEW MINUTES LATER, his mother reappears from the bedroom, closing the door behind her. She takes a deep breath and looks at me.

"HE CONFESSED."

MY BREATH CATCHES in my throat. "What?"

· · ·

"I told you he did it. That kid can't tell the truth for nothing. I don't know what I'm going to do with him," she says, shaking her head as she walks into the kitchen and pours a glass of wine right in the middle of the afternoon. I take that as my cue to leave.

I run to look out the front window for the tenth time, but no one is in the driveway yet. The timer dings on the stove, so I jog back to check on the spaghetti sauce that's simmering in a pot. The chocolate chip cookies have just finished, so I put them on top of the stove and then run back to the window.

I'm now positive I've never been so nervous.

Ethan offered to bring Harper to the house so that our first meeting can be in a "safe" place for both of us, although my childhood home doesn't always bring back warm and cozy memories. I am determined to change my memories by making it a home for the both of us.

I wonder if she'll call me Aunt Indy or Mom. Neither sounds right. I have nieces and a nephew in Seattle, but they don't know me and don't really call me anything.

Sometimes it makes me feel like a bad person that I don't have a close bond with my sister and her family, but then I remember that I've never been invited to visit. Maybe Amy is waiting for me to make the first move, but I highly doubt it.

. . .

I RUN BACK to the stove and turn the sauce down just as I hear a car door slam. Instead of standing in the window like some kind of nut job, I stand behind the solid front door, waiting for the inevitable bell. When it rings, I wait for a few moments, not wanting to appear too eager, before I open it.

BEHIND THE SOLID door is a full glass one, and through its clear pane I see her for the first time. She's the spitting image of my brother - tall for her age, lanky, angry face that I wasn't expecting. She doesn't want to be here, that much is evident. I imagine that she'll never be a great poker player with a face like that.

SHE HAS fire engine red hair and freckles across her nose, two things that my brother definitely *didn't* have. I wonder what her mother looked like.

"HELLO," I say, which seems highly inadequate for the situation. "Please come in." Why do I sound like I'm welcoming guests at Buckingham Palace instead of into my small brick ranch in Peach Valley?

ETHAN GIVES me a forced smile with a hint of a warning in it. I cock my head as he pushes Harper into the house past me, and I notice that her arm is hanging limp beside her as she drags her pink suitcase. She looks like someone is marching her to the death chamber.

WE GO to the living room and sit down. I bought the house

furnished since I didn't have time to go furniture shopping, but I've already grown to loathe the sleek, modern furniture that currently inhabits the living room. The sofa is white and looks like something out the *Jetson's* cartoon from my childhood, and the matching tables are glass and chrome. I feel like I'm in the waiting room of a hospital.

"NICE COUCH," Harper says under her breath, sarcasm seeping from every word. She drops her suitcase in the middle of the floor and then stands at the back door, staring out into the yard.

"THANKS. I HATE IT TOO," I say back. I see her slightly turn her head, cutting her eyes in my direction, but so far she hasn't made eye contact with me. I look at Ethan and he shrugs his shoulders. "Can I speak with you for a moment? In private?" I say to him. He nods.

"HARPER, we're going to step out onto the front porch for a minute. Why don't you take some time to look around?" he says.

"HAVE FUN TALKING ABOUT ME," she mutters as we walk through the foyer and out the front door.

CLOSING the wood door behind me in the hopes of privacy, I cross my arms and glare at Ethan. "You said she was a good kid."

. . .

"SHE IS A GOOD KID, Indy. I've never seen her act this way."

"GREAT. LUCKY ME." It feels like someone is drilling a hole in the top of my head.

"COME ON NOW. She just lost her father, and she's been bounced around for weeks now. Give the kid a break."

"WHAT HAVE I DONE?" I say to myself, tilting my head back against the brick and sighing. "I had a great life in Charleston."

ETHAN PUTS his hands on my shoulders. "Indy, she needs you. You're a therapist. You're her aunt. And now you're her mother. Don't give up before you even get started."

I DON'T KNOW what I expected, but it wasn't this. I guess I thought she'd be thankful to see me, her long lost aunt, and maybe she'd run into my waiting arms and smile. Right now, I feel like frisking her for weapons and sleeping with one eye open.

"I'M GOING to hit the road. I've got a real estate closing this afternoon…" he says, looking at the time on his phone.

"WHAT? You're leaving? Just like that?"

. . .

RACHEL HANNA

ETHAN CHUCKLES. "What do you want me to do, Indy? She's your child now. You kind of have to figure this out on your own, like the rest of us. Kids don't come with manuals, unfortunately." He squeezes the top of my arm before walking down the three front steps. "You've got this, Indy Stone... superhero."

"SANDERS."

"SURE. WHATEVER YOU SAY..." he sings back to me as he walks to his car and drives away, leaving me with the angriest ten-year old in Peach Valley.

I TAKE another moment to gather myself before walking back into the house. Harper is still standing at the back door, arms crossed. Maybe she gets that stance from me.

EVEN THOUGH I'VE counseled many children, and their parents, I realize that this is a completely different situation. There are feelings involved that can't be swept under the rug. Objectivity is not a part of this at all.

"I'M SO glad you're here Harper. I know losing your father has been difficult..."

"HOW WOULD you know anything about my father?" she says through gritted teeth. I can see her fists balled up by her sides.

40

. . .

"HE WAS MY BROTHER," I say, reminding her as if she doesn't know.

"MY FATHER DIDN'T HAVE anyone but me," she says softly. "Everyone else abandoned him."

AND NOW I SEE IT. She's been fed a lot of misinformation in her short life, seeing things from only my brother's distorted mind. Her anger is righteous, but misdirected.

"SWEETIE," I say, but immediately want to retract my words when I see her tiny jaw tighten, "I loved my brother. But sometimes there is history there that prevents us from allowing people to be in our lives..."

SHE'S TEN. I'm talking over her head.

SHE SLOWLY TURNS and finally looks at me, the first time we've made eye contact. "When you really love someone, you don't leave them. No matter what." Without another word, she picks up her suitcase and walks down the hall, going instinctively into the room I picked for her and shutting the door.

"ETHAN, I want to see my brother's will," I say, storming

straight into his office past his well-meaning, but woefully inadequate, secretary.

ETHAN COVERS the mouthpiece of his landline phone - a relic from times gone by - and shushes me. "Tim, I'm going to have to call you back. Right. Okay. Talk soon." He places the phone back on the receiver and stands up. "Indy, this is a place of business."

"YEAH, I don't care right now. I need to see my brother's will."

"WHY?"

"BECAUSE I NEED ANSWERS. Why would he want me to raise his daughter? I don't understand. She's angry at me, and he's obviously told her some very distorted 'facts' over the years."

"HIS WILL DOESN'T EXPLAIN, Indy. There's no mention of a reason. I promise."

I FALL DOWN into a chair and swing my head down between my knees, hanging there like a limp puppet. Realizing that I'm not acting like the professional woman I am, I pop back up, almost giving myself enough of a head rush to pass out.

"THIS JUST MAKES no sense to me, Ethan."

. . .

HE WALKS AROUND and sits on the edge of his desk in front of me. "Look, I know you and Danny had a very complicated past, but maybe he just knew you'd be good for Harper. He kept up with you, Indy."

"KEPT UP WITH ME? What does that mean?"

"THE FEW TIMES WE SPOKE, he told me you lived in Charleston and that you were a therapist."

"HE DID? That's weird. How would he know that?"

"SOCIAL MEDIA?"

"I'M NOT ON SOCIAL MEDIA."

HE LOOKS at me as if I have two heads. "You're not on any social media?"

"NO. I prefer to socialize with actual human beings." I realize I'm being a huge pain in the butt right now, but I want to stand up and stomp my feet and maybe throw myself on the floor to have a full-on adult temper tantrum. Or maybe I can just drink some wine when I get home.

. . .

HOME. The place where the angry redhead shall ignore me completely.

"SHE HATES ME, Ethan. I mean really hates me."

"INDY, it's going to be okay. You know kids go through phases like this, and she's grieving. Give her time. Give yourself time."

I TAKE a deep breath and nod. "Thanks for listening to me rant. Again." I stand up and swing my purse over my shoulder.

"CAN I give you one piece of advice?" he asks before I leave his office.

"I WILL TAKE ALL the advice you have."

"WHAT HARPER NEEDS to know is that you honor the part of her father that is inside of her. She needs to know that he was loved, at least by someone other than her. She needs to know that it's acceptable to talk about him, and to have loved him with all of her heart. If you can give her pieces of him that she never had, I think she'll come around."

I SMILE. "Maybe you should be the therapist."

As I sit on the front steps waiting for Harper to get home from school, I close my eyes and hear the leaves of the fig tree rustling on front of me. The tree is bigger than ever now, and I don't know how anyone would safely get the figs from the top of it.

Still, it brings back memories that I can't shake.

August 1987

"I'll be back soon," my mother says as I stand on the front walkway. She's been acting awfully mysterious lately with "meetings", which makes no sense because she's a stay at home mother and not some kind of business executive. When I ask where she's going, she mumbles and leaves as soon as possible. The whole thing is making me uneasy.

When she pulls away, I'm left home alone because my sister is already at a friend's house and my brother... well, who knows where he is? He has been gone more than he's been home all summer, but no one is saying where he is exactly.

I sit down on the bottom step and look toward Dawson's house. It's been days since the fire truck incident, and I won't talk to him. I keep my blinds closed in my room, and I shoved my strobe light to the back of my closet. It just doesn't have the same appeal as it once did. One day he came to my house, but I made my Mom tell him I was taking a bath.

I DON'T KNOW *why I'm so upset with him. I guess because he lied to me, and we've always told each other the truth. I mean, we've only known each other a few weeks, but I thought he was my friend. I never thought he'd look me in the face and lie. It made my heart hurt.*

I CLOSE *my eyes and start to sing my favorite Madonna song. She's a little crazy and wild, but I like her. I wish I could just be myself without worrying what everyone thought. Mom says she looks like a prostitute, but I have no idea what one looks like. I just think she looks cool.*

"YOU HAVE A GOOD VOICE, INDY," *I hear someone say. Startled, I jump up and start looking around. "Over here."*

I NOTICE *the leaves rustling in our large fig tree, and then I realize that I know the voice. Dawson. I can just see his eyes barely poking out when he waves a hand for me to join him in the tree. I cross my arms and shake my head.*

"No," *I say and turn to go up the stairs.*

"PLEASE, *Indy. I can't come out or my mother might see me. I'm supposed to be in my room, but I climbed out my window."*

. . .

"WHY ARE you so focused on getting in trouble?" I genuinely want to know what makes him take these risks.

"PLEASE COME HERE."

THE SOUND of his voice makes me turn back and walk toward the fig tree. I shoot a glance toward his house to make sure his mother isn't outside and then I slide into the tree too. Thank goodness the huge family of bees seems to be gone now that the weather is cooling off.

HE'S SITTING on one of the bigger branches and reaches a hand down to pull me up. I put my sneaker on one of the lower branches and take his hand as he hoists me upward. He's stronger than he looks. Still, I don't make eye contact. I'm determined to stay mad at him.

"WHAT DO YOU WANT, DAWSON?" I ask, trying to cross my arms again but too afraid I might fall out of the tree if I do.

"I'M sorry I lied to you, Indy. I need you to know that I didn't plan to do that. It's just..."

"JUST WHAT? What possible reason can you give for lying to me?"

"I WAS TRYING to get her attention," he says so softly that I barely hear him.

47

. . .

"WHAT?"

HE SHAKES a stray chunk of his thick brown hair from his eyes. "I wanted her to pay attention, Indy. I know it sounds crazy, but she ignores me most of the time. When I make big mistakes, at least she notices me. But this time I think I went too far."

"YA THINK?" I say sarcastically. "That's twisted, Dawson. Doing bad stuff for attention?"

"I DIDN'T KNOW you were coming over. Then I felt like I was screwed. I just couldn't tell the truth."

"YOU COULD HAVE. You chose not to."

HE REACHES out and grabs my hand so tightly that it feels like he's drowning and I'm his life jacket. I look at him, and I feel something. I don't know what it is, but I feel like a million butterflies are bouncing around every corner of my stomach and my face feels hot. He stares at me, a look of pain in his eyes, and I want to take it away from him. I just don't know how.

"I THINK my mom doesn't want me around anymore, Indy," he whispers, as if she's standing outside of the tree.

. . .

"DAWSON, *I'm sure that's not true...*"

"I'M A BURDEN TO HER. *She told me so last night.*"

"SHE CALLED YOU A BURDEN?"

"WELL, *I heard her tell her friend that on the phone. Look, I don't know what's going to happen, but I just had to make sure that you knew that I would never hurt you on purpose. You're my best friend and I... Well, I wouldn't lie to you on purpose like that." He's still gripping my hand firmly, and I'm afraid of the sadness I might feel when he lets it go.*

"YOU'RE *my best friend too, Dawson," I say. Truly, he feels like a level above friend. I don't know what to call that level. "This will all work out. I promise. Things are going to be okay." Even as I say it, I know it's not true. I have no power to change his family problems... or my own. We've only talked a little bit about my family, specifically my brother. My mother has warned me against telling people too much because she says that everyone just wants to hear your dirty laundry and then talk bad about you at their dinner table.*

HE SMILES SADLY, *and I get this weird feeling that he knows more than he's saying. I don't push, because I know what it's like to need to keep some things secret.*

"THANK *you for being there for me, Indy," he says, and before I know what's happening, he leans over and kisses me softly on my lips. Time freezes and all I can feel is the softness of his lips against mine. He doesn't move them like I see in the movies, but just presses them there for a long moment. I decide I never want to leave this tree. I just want to stay here with Dawson's lips pressed against mine until the day I die.*

BUT THEN, before I can open my eyes - which I've closed tightly to enjoy the moment - he pulls back and jumps from the tree. By the time I realize what's happening, I see him running toward his house as the sun sets in the Georgia sky.

～

HARPER GETS off the bus right on time, but she simply walks past me into the house like I'm not sitting there on the porch in front of her. I take in another deep breath of the crisp fall air before I walk into the house.

HARPER IS IN THE KITCHEN, standing in front of the open refrigerator door. She doesn't appear to be reaching for anything, just looking.

"I BOUGHT some of those frozen peanut butter and jelly sandwiches if you'd like to have one. I can thaw one out…"

"NO THANKS."

I MOVE past her in the long galley kitchen and open the

cabinet beside the laundry room door. "I also bought some canned ravioli…"

"I'LL JUST EAT AN APPLE," she says, grabbing one from the new fruit bowl I've placed on the kitchen table, before walking straight to her room and shutting the door.

SUDDENLY, I question myself. Can I really do this? Will this kid ever have a normal conversation with me?

MY LIFE WAS SO simple just a couple of weeks ago. I lived in a nice condo right on the water in Charleston. The biggest decision I had each day was whether I wanted hot tea or a latte at the local coffee shop. I had a full roster of counseling clients who looked to me for life advice and paid me well for dispensing it.

NOW, I'm basically begging a ten-year old kid to eat something and being ignored in my own house. Yep, living the dream.

I SIT DOWN at the kitchen table and look around the room, trying to remember the tacky wallpaper we used to have when I was a kid. It was a mixture of golden yellows and vomit green, yet somehow my mother thought it was a stunning display of interior design. Our floor had been covered in vinyl tiles that were a deep green color. It's funny how you hate things as a child, but find yourself craving the familiarity of them as an adult. I secretly wonder if that old vinyl is under the newer hardwood laminate floors, but decide against ripping them up to find out.

Even though this isn't the table I grew up with, I can remember those family dinners we had every Sunday. The times when everything seemed good, and the times when I was well aware that my family unit had irreparably broken down.

It wasn't just my brother, although I will always believe he was the catalyst, the unpredictable flame that lit the match. It was as if a variety of events unknown to me converged to form one of the worst days of my life.

CHAPTER 4

*A*ugust 1987

"I bet you can't do a one-handed cartwheel," I challenge Tabitha. She's definitely not the most agile of my friends, so it's a pretty safe bet that she's going to face plant if she even attempts it.

"I'm not stupid, Indy. You just want to watch me fall!"

We both giggle and fall onto the grass in my front yard. It's getting darker by the minute which means my Dad will pull into the driveway from work soon. He has one of those cool work vans that's filled with a lot of stuff I don't understand. As a mechanic, he says it's okay that his van is the messiest place on Earth. I don't think Mom agrees.

"Indigo, dinner will be ready in about fifteen minutes. Come on in and get cleaned up," my mother calls from the front porch. She isn't smiling, and she's barely looking at me before she turns and walks back inside. Normally, she at least speaks to Tabitha.

"See you tomorrow," Tabitha says, taking a cue from my mother.

I decide to do another cartwheel before going inside. When I pop back upright, I glance at Dawson's house. I haven't seen him in a few days, since our kiss in the tree. In fact, I haven't seen his mother either.

"Indigo! In the house." My mother is stern now, the stress apparent on her face.

"When is Dad coming home?" I ask, wondering why I can't stay outside and wait for him like I always do.

"Your Dad is on the phone."

*"On the phone? Why?" I'm very confused at this point. My Dad doesn't normally call home. He's supposed to **be** home. She doesn't answer and walks back in the house, so I follow her.*

The phone is sitting on the kitchen table, it's extended length cord pooled on the floor. My mother walks to the other end of the kitchen and appears to be doing something.

"Dad? When are you coming home?" I ask.

There's a pause and then what sounds like a sniffle. "I'm not, honey."

"What do you mean you're not?" My stomach is starting to hurt like the time I got food poisoning from that bad potato salad at the church picnic.

"Indy, your mother has asked me for a divorce."

Divorce? No. That can't be right. Other people get divorced. Not my parents. Not my family. My parents never fight. Everything was fine last night. Wasn't it? I rack my brain trying to remember the last time we were together as a family. I can't remember anything for some reason.

"No, she hasn't. You must have misunderstood, Daddy. Right, Mom? He can come home..."

My mother is standing there, not making eye contact with me, biting her lip. Her chin is jutted out like she's trying to keep her head above water.

"No, Indy. Daddy can't come home. But you'll see him every weekend..."

I look at her as if she has two heads and then turn back toward the window facing our backyard. The sun has set, and all I can see in the darkened kitchen is my own reflection in the window, tears starting to pool in my lower eyelids.

"Daddy, please come home. I'm sure ya'll can work this out..." I don't even know what that means. Adults are so confusing.

"Honey, I can't," he says through a shaky voice. "I'll call you tomorrow, okay?" Before I can respond, he hangs up and I'm left with a dial tone piercing my ear drum. I slowly hang up the phone knowing that my mother stands behind me, waiting for some kind of reaction. I feel so betrayed right now.

"Why did you do this?" I finally ask softly without meeting her eyes.

"Indy, this is an adult issue. Your Dad and I decided..."

"No! No! You decided. I know he didn't want this!" I run out of the kitchen and into my bedroom, locking the door behind me before falling face first onto my bed.

Once every tear seems to have fallen from my red, puffy eyes, I turn onto my back and stare at the ceiling of my bedroom. And I decide the only thing that will make me feel better is seeing Dawson.

I hear my mother on the kitchen phone, deep in conversation with her best friend most likely. I creep into my sister's room because her window is close to the ground, and I slip out into the night air.

It's getting cooler now, but not by much. Georgia tends to have sweltering summers that seem to last for way too long.

I see lights on in Dawson's house, although not in his bedroom. After tapping on his window several times without getting a response, I stand there to consider my options.

I can go back home and cry all night alone, or I can chance it by knocking on his door and hoping his mother takes pity on me enough to let him come outside and talk to me.

I summon my courage and ring the bell, which elicits barking from their small, yappy dog. Finally, his mother appears in the doorway, a cigarette in her hand and a scowl on her face.

"Indy." She says it like that's a complete sentence.

"Hi, ma'am. Is Dawson able to come out and talk? It's just that something happened and I really wanted to talk to him..." Now, I'm babbling.

She purses her lips. "Dawson doesn't live here anymore, Indy." She starts to close the door, but I push back and she looks surprised.

"Excuse me? What do you mean he doesn't live here?"

She looks behind her, and I notice Dawson's little sister - who has special needs - and that grungy man sitting on the sofa. He's drinking a beer while the little girl colors, and the sight of him makes me cringe for some reason. I don't like that guy at all. Pulling the door behind her, she steps out onto the porch with me.

"Look, Indy, I appreciate that you like Dawson. I'd hoped that having a new friend might get him to make better choices, but it hasn't."

"Where is Dawson?"

"He's at a home for wayward boys in North Carolina."

"What?" I don't really understand what that means, but it doesn't sound good.

"Dawson isn't coming back here, Indy. He'll be living there for at least six months, and I'm moving in with my boyfriend this weekend."

"Can I write to him at least?" I ask, a begging tone to my voice.

"No. He can't have any outside contact. He needs a lot of help, Indy. That boy has problems." With that, she steps back into the house and closes the door, sliding the chain lock as if I'm going to kick the door in with my scrawny legs.

For a moment, I stand there on the porch as it starts to mist rain. I can't believe Dawson is gone. And my Dad is gone. And I haven't seen my brother in weeks. I feel more alone right now than I ever have in my life.

I WALK into the lobby of the school out of breath and concerned. When the counselor called me and said she needed to talk to me about Harper, my heart dropped. I remember when my mother used to get those calls about Danny.

In fact, one time the principal himself had called my mother because my brother had locked him in his office and wouldn't let him out. At the time, I thought it was kind of funny. His principal was a bit of a dork. But later I realized how serious it had been and how scared that poor little man must have been when my gigantic, drug addled brother had threatened him.

But my mother had taken it in stride. She marched over to the school, settled my brother down and apologized to the principal. In today's world, my brother would have been all over the news coverage and arrested. Times were just different then.

"Hi. I'm Indy Sanders. Mrs. Calloway called about my... niece... Harper."

The woman gives me what could only be described as a sympathetic smile and nods. "Yes, let me tell her that you're here. Please have a seat."

She points to a small waiting area. The office is glass enclosed, so I spend a few moments watching children mill about in the hallway. This is a newer school and not the one I attended all those years ago. It's much more state-of-the-art with computers and bright lights and shiny, peppy teachers with high blond pony tails and cheerleader looks. All of my teachers had looked like they were one step away from being cast in *The Walking Dead*.

"Ms. Sanders? You can come back now," the woman says.

57

She leads me down a short hallway into a room with a small conference table. "Mrs. Calloway will be in shortly."

A few moments later, a rotund woman with short gray hair on her head and black hair on her chin - that I'm trying hard to ignore - walks in and sits down with a grunt. Not even a handshake. This can't be good.

"Hello, Ms. Sanders. I'm Evelyn Calloway, the counselor here at Peach Valley Elementary School."

"Nice to meet you."

"Well, I wish we were meeting under better circumstances."

"Oh?"

"We're having some... issues... with Harper."

"Issues?" This comes as news to me mainly because Ethan and Lisa have both raved about what a great kid she is. Of course, I haven't seen evidence of this yet.

"Well, yes. Ever since her father died... and you became her guardian... Harper has been out of sorts, it seems."

"Okay..." I realize in this moment that I am ill equipped to be a parent, at least a parent who has been thrown into the pre-teen angsty years. "How so?"

"Today she pulled the fire alarm and then escaped out the back door of the school and into the woods. Her favorite teacher was the only one who could coax her out."

"Sounds like you need better locks on your doors," I say without thinking.

She takes in a long breath through her ample nose and blinks slowly. "Mrs. Sanders, I would hope you'd take this problem seriously. We're very close to suspending your niece."

Suspension? I suddenly realize that if they suspend her, I will be homeschooling her due to the lack of private school options in Peach Valley. And that definitely won't work.

"What else has she done?"

"Two days ago she cut another girl's ponytail off. And at the end of last week, she hid Mrs. Appleton's quizzes for an entire day, causing her to be late inputting her grades…"

"Okay. I get it. No need to go on. What would you propose I do, Mrs. Calloway?"

"Well, with all due respect, she's your child now. And I understand you're a therapist?" She says it in a high pitched voice as if she wants me to prove this fact by showing her my degree.

"As you can imagine, we're going through a bit of a transition, Mrs. Calloway."

"I understand. But we must protect our school, our teachers and most importantly, our students."

"Of course. I'll talk to Harper this evening when she gets home, and we'll work something out. I'm sorry she's been such an issue." I stand up and start heading for the door.

"You know, I was thinking you might want to talk to her favorite teacher. He seems to understand her better than anyone."

At first, I'm surprised it's a male, but then it makes sense to me because she was raised by her father alone. Maybe she's just more comfortable around men.

"Okay. Is he here?"

"No. Mr. Woods was out today, but he'll be back tomorrow. His planning hour is at eleven. Can you come then?"

I nod my head and tell her thank you for her time before I head to my car, wondering the whole time whether this situation will ever be salvageable.

I STAND in my new yard and stare at the gigantic fig tree. It really is amazing how large it is, taking up a good third of the whole front yard. Still, I've got to do some pruning soon because it's starting to block the view of the driveway.

"Indy! Hi! Welcome back to the neighborhood," Lisa says as she power walks by with a big smile.

"Oh, hey, Lisa. Do you have a minute?"

She takes out her earphones and jogs over to me. "Sure. What's up?"

"Mrs. Calloway called me to the school today… about Harper." Lisa nods and bites her bottom lip.

"Yeah. She seems to be having some issues lately, and it's so unlike her."

"Mrs. Calloway suggested I talk to her favorite teacher. Mr. Woods?"

Lisa grins. "Yes. Mr. Woods," she says before taking in a deep breath. "He's new to the school this year and absolutely gorgeous. Thick, dark, wavy hair. Eyelashes for days. Muscular…"

"Earth to Lisa," I say, waving my hand in front of her face as she stares into space, obviously looking at this Mr. Woods character in her mind.

"Sorry. It's just that we never see men like him in Peach Valley."

"Well, I'm not interested in a man right now. I'm focused on getting Harper stable. So you think I should talk to him?"

"Absolutely. From what I've heard, he's been the only one who could talk to her. He coaxed her back out of the woods."

"She definitely isn't talking to me," I say. "After she got off the bus today, she locked herself in her room saying she had homework. That was two hours ago." I sit down on the steps and Lisa sits next to me.

"This has to be hard for you, Indy."

I laugh sadly. "Very hard. I have such mixed emotions about this place. This house. Even this tree."

"The fig tree?"

"Yeah."

"Why?"

I pause. No one really knew about my friendship with Dawson, and I kind of want to keep it that way. It's like my little secret, a part of my history that no one can touch or taint with their own opinions.

"It was just always here. Through it all."

"Well, I'd better get home. Johnny likes to have dinner on the table at seven, so I've got to start cooking."

"Johnny?"

"Oh, I married Johnny Deeds. Do you remember him?"

I struggle not to laugh. Johnny Deeds was the town gigolo back in the day, or at least that's what my sister always said.

"I do remember him."

She smiles. "He settled down, Indy. He teaches Sunday School, and we have two little girls that he'd die for."

Apparently some things do change in Peach Valley.

WHEN I WALK BACK into the house, Harper is sitting on the living room sofa to my surprise. She's watching some teenager type show on the television while staring down at her iPod. I'm determined to have a conversation with her.

"Hey. Whatcha watchin'? I say, trying to sound a lot cooler than I am.

She turns and scowls at me. "A TV show."

"Look, Harper, we need to talk..."

"No. We don't." She turns off the TV and starts to stand up. I touch her arm and she pulls back.

"Yes, we do. We can't go on living in the same house and not speaking. I realize this is a tough transition for you, but I want to make this work. I want the best for you."

"Oh, like you wanted the best for my Daddy?"

That stings. I wonder how much she knows about what her father did to the family. And would she even understand at her age? Would she care?

"Please, sit back down and let's talk. Okay?"

She sucks in a shaky, angry breath and sits down, not looking at me. But it's a start.

"Yes, your father was estranged from his family for a long time. But I'm not going to bad mouth him, especially not now…"

"Now that he'd dead, you mean? But you mistreated him while he was alive!"

"Harper, that's simply not true. Let me ask you something. Have you ever had a kid at school who wasn't nice to you?"

She cocks her head at me in confusion. "Yeah."

"What was their name?"

"Dylan."

"And what did he do?"

"It was in third grade. He pulled my hair and stole my lunch. And he would sing this song 'I'd rather be dead than have red on my head'."

"He sounds like a real jerk." I kind of want to hunt him down.

"He was. He moved at the end of the year, thank goodness."

"How did you get through the year with him?"

"I ignored him. I told him to leave me alone."

"And did that work?"

"Sometimes. Not always."

"So you tried to remove him from your life because he wasn't nice to you, right?"

"Yesss…." she says, still unsure of what I'm saying.

"Harper, I loved your father. He was my only brother. But he wasn't very nice when he was a teenager. He had some…

problems... that made him angry. We all tried to help him, but he wasn't getting better. I chose to protect myself. Does that make sense?"

She stares at me, her jaw tight and her lips pursed. "He was a good man! Don't you talk bad about my Daddy!" She shoots straight up out of her seat and crosses her arms with her back to me.

"Harper, I wish I'd known him as a man. I'm sure he was a wonderful father to you."

"You never even tried. You just left him. You left us. We had nobody." I can hear her choking back tears.

"Honey, I didn't even know where Danny was or that he had a daughter. If I'd known..." I wonder to myself whether I'd have even reached out then. So many years had passed, and I didn't want drama in my life.

"Every Christmas, we had this little tiny tree in our apartment and a couple of presents. All of my friends at school had big family dinners and grandparents who visited with piles of presents. I had a frozen dinner with my Dad while we watched Disney movies."

My breath catches. The vision of my brother, big and strong, sitting in a little apartment trying to make Christmas special for his daughter just about breaks my heart into pieces.

"They tried to take me away from him once, but my Daddy fought for me and he won."

"They? You mean the authorities?"

"Yeah. But my Daddy told me that when you love somebody, you never give up. He said he'd never give up on me either, no matter what I did."

I look down at my feet, unsure of what to say next. All of my training never prepared me for a moment like this. How do you make a child understand decisions you made as a child yourself?

"Your Daddy was right," I hear myself saying. "You don't walk out on people you love, and I'm not going to walk out on you, Harper. We're going to get through this together."

She turns to me, tears streaming down her face. "I don't want anybody but my Daddy," she says as she walks past me into her bedroom and shuts the door.

CHAPTER 5

$\mathcal{I}$ don't know why I feel so nervous. Maybe because I've had two cups of coffee this morning. Or maybe it's because I got three hours of sleep after my talk with Harper last night.

She finally came out of her room after dinner and made a plate for herself before taking it back to her room and shutting the door. I gave her space. Maybe I was really giving myself space. I felt like my words would fail me, so I chose not to chance it.

"Ms. Sanders?" I hear a woman say from behind me. "I'll show you to Mr. Woods' room now."

I follow her out of the office and down a long hallway to the last door on the left. The halls are quiet except for the occasional child passing by.

"You can wait here. He should be back any minute," she says, pulling the door closed behind her.

I look around and notice mostly indications that he's a history teacher. Globes. History posters. Historical books. I think back to my own school days. I was a good student, a nerd by today's standards. I loved school and the escape it provided me from a volatile time in my life. Maybe Harper feels the same.

"Sorry to have kept you waiting, Ms. Sanders," a male voice says from behind me as I stand reading a poster about Benjamin Franklin. Just the voice alone is sexy, smooth, husky. I can already imagine what Lisa was talking about.

I turn around and have to steady myself on the desk next to me. His face. Tanned. Beautiful white-toothed smile. Strong jawline with hints of stubble. Thick, wavy dark hair.

Dawson.

"Oh my God," is all I manage to say. I wonder for a moment if he remembers me, but his face seems to say he does.

"Indy?" he says softly, as if he's looking at a ghost.

We just stand there with about five feet between us, each of us staring at the other. It feels like we stand this way for an hour, but at the same time only seconds.

"Dawson." I say his name because I haven't been able to say it in many years.

"You're Harper's mother?"

"I am now."

He clears his throat and steps toward me. "It's so good to see you," he says, pulling me into a tight embrace. He's strong now, a man and not a boy. He still smells familiar for some reason. The hug is quick and then he pulls back and shuffles his feet for a moment. "Why don't we sit down?"

I find a chair across from his small desk and we again stare at each other for a moment.

"Right. So, about Harper… how can I help?"

I'm taken aback by how quickly he jumps to the subject of Harper, but realize it only makes sense as that is the reason I'm here.

"Mrs. Calloway suggested I talk to her favorite teacher…

which is you... but I didn't know it was you... how did I never know your last name?"

He smiles. God, he's gorgeous. Model material. I imagine every mother with a kid in his class comes to as many parent/teacher conferences as possible. Trying to not be obvious, I quickly glance at his left hand but see no wedding ring.

"We were kids, Indy. Last names didn't matter much back then, I guess."

"Of course." We *were* kids. I highly doubt his few weeks around me made a lasting impression on his life.

"So, about Harper. She's a good kid. She just really needs to be heard. Maybe you could try telling her some good memories you have of her father?"

My eyes grow wide and I look down. "I'll have to think about that. I think I've blocked quite a bit out about that time in my life."

He bites his lip. "About me too?"

I look at him for a long moment. "No. I remember some things very vividly."

There's a thick tension hanging between us for a moment. "I can't believe you're sitting right in front of me."

I let out the breath I've been holding since I saw him. "Me either. I thought I'd never see you again."

He smiles and then nervously shuffles some papers on his desk. "Listen, I'd love to catch up with you some time. Maybe we could grab dinner?"

I want to say yes. It's just catching up. But a part of me feels danger, and my sole focus needs to be Harper right now. Not opening old wounds or unlocking distant memories.

"Maybe."

He furrows his brows but then smiles slightly. "Okay

then. Well, if I can be of more help, or if I can talk to Harper with you… or for you… just let me know."

He stands up as if he's inviting me to leave. "It was nice to see you again, Dawson."

"You too, Indy. Truly a nice surprise."

He winks at me before he sits back down and starts looking at papers on his desk, and my heart thuds as I walk out the door.

I'M NOT A NATURAL COOK. I've never claimed to be a chef. But I'm pretty dang proud of my accomplishment this evening. I was able to follow a recipe I found online and cook a nice pot roast with vegetables and biscuits. So the biscuits came out of one of those cans that almost explodes and scares you. Who cares? They're still edible biscuits, even if not homemade.

"Harper? Is that you?" I call as the front door opens. I hear a grunt that indicates it's her and not some ax murderer, although I might check her hand for weapons just in case.

I walk out into the living room, and she's sitting in the chair next to the TV. She doesn't look so good.

"Are you okay?"

"No. I feel terrible," she says softly.

"What's wrong?" I ask, kneeling in front of her.

"My throat hurts and my nose is stuffy."

For the first time, I feel that motherly instinct coming over me. I want to protect her. I don't want her to be in pain.

"Come on, kid. Let's head to the doctor," I say, taking her hand and pulling her upright. "Wait. Do you have a doctor here?"

She looks at me like I'm a moron. "Um, yeah. Of course I do. Dr. Dothan."

I grab my purse and my phone and we load up in my car in search of Dr. Dothan's office.

THE NEWS ISN'T GREAT. Harper has strep and gets antibiotics. I've got instructions to give her warm soup and ice chips and basically whatever she wants for the next forty-eight hours while she stays home from school.

A part of me wants to care for her, but the other part of me is terrified that these will be the longest two days of my life.

Once we get home, I make her a can of chicken and rice soup with some ginger ale and put her to bed. When I look in there an hour later, she's out like a light.

Deciding that I need some fresh air, I leave her a note in case she wakes up - which is unlikely - and I walk outside into the front yard. For some reason, stress makes me want to walk. Sometimes I've walked for miles before I realize what I'm doing.

This evening, I'm not walking far. Just to the end of the street. I want to peek across the main road and get a look at Tabitha's house. I haven't seen her since we were kids, and I don't even know where she lives now. Maybe I'll check into that soon.

When I get to the end of the street, I strain my eyes across the road and see her house. It still looks much the same since it was an all brick ranch, but the shutters are now black when they used to be cream colored. And the once small trees in her yard are now taller and more mature. Life goes on even when we aren't watching.

Worried about going too far from Harper, I turn to head back toward the house. As if history loves to repeat itself, I find myself sneezing in the exact same spot as I did when I met Dawson all those years ago. Something about that spot, I guess. On instinct, I stop and wait to hear "bless you" and then laugh at myself for reminiscing as I start walking again.

"Do you need to see an allergy doctor or something?"

I turn to see Dawson leaning against the railing of the front porch of his old rental house. The sight of him standing there takes my breath away for a moment.

"What are you doing there?"

"I live here, Indy."

My mouth drops open without my approval. "What? Since when?"

"Moved in a few days ago." He slowly strolls toward me with an impressive stride. A manly stride. It's weird seeing him all grown up.

"Renting?"

He laughs. "No. I'm a big boy now. Bought it all by myself about six months ago. The rehab work just got finished last week."

Now we're face to face, standing at the edge of his yard. "But why?"

"Because this was the last home I ever really had. It was the last place I was truly happy."

That statement makes me sad, yet happy at the same time because I was a part of his life then. "You didn't seem so happy back then."

I start walking and he follows, as we slowly walk toward my house. It occurs to me that he's free now. He can walk out of his house and walk to mine without his mother punishing him.

We sit down on the railroad ties at the edge of my property. "I wasn't very happy most of the time. Only when I was with you." His voice is soft and vulnerable and immensely attractive.

"Did you know… that I moved back?" I ask hesitantly.

He chuckles. "No, Indy. I didn't. This was all fate's fault."

"Fate?"

"Do you know that I started looking for you as soon as social media was invented?" he asks. I laugh, but then realize that he's being serious.

"You did? Really?"

"Yep. For years I would check for your name, but nothing. I guess you got married?"

"I did. And I wasn't really into social media. I prefer face to face interactions."

"Well," he says softly, his face inches from mine, "we're certainly face to face now."

I clear my throat nervously, visions of our one and only kiss in the fig tree zipping around my head. And for some inexplicable reason, I stand up quickly to escape the memories and his presence. All these years I've wondered about him. Missed him. And now he's literally at my doorstep and I want to run.

"I… need to check on Harper. She's been sick with strep…"

"Oh no. I'm sorry to hear that. Tell her I hope she feels better. And if you need anything… Well, you know where I am," he says with a wink as he stands up.

"Right," I say, turning because there's a smile spreading across my face that I don't want him to see. "Good night."

"Will you be dancing tonight?"

"Very funny, Dawson…" I say in a singsongy voice.

I hear him laughing as I walk up the stairs to my house. When I peek around the corner of the porch post, he's gone.

As Harper sleeps in the next room, I stare at my cell phone with dread. It's dinner time in Seattle, so it's definitely not too late to call, but I just don't want to do it. Still, she's my sister, and I need to tell her about Danny.

"Hello?" Her voice is chipper; nothing like the sister I grew up with.

"Hi, Amy. It's Indy."

Long pause. "Oh. Hey. What's up?"

"I know you're probably surprised to hear from me."

"I am. But it's good to hear your voice." Didn't expect that last comment.

"Good to hear yours too." Definitely didn't expect to hear that come from my mouth.

"I need to tell you some difficult news."

"Okay…"

"Danny… passed away."

"What?"

"A few weeks ago. I'm back in Peach Valley."

"Why?" I can hear a bit of a crack in her voice.

"Because I bought our old house back."

"You did what? But you hated that house. Why would you go back?"

"Because Danny had a daughter that we didn't know about, and he left guardianship to me, Amy."

She doesn't say anything for a long moment. "Wow."

"Yeah, that was exactly my reaction. And let's just say that she isn't happy that I'm her new mommy."

Amy laughs. "Well, if she's anything like Danny…"

"In some ways, she definitely is. But she's so beautiful, Amy. Red hair and freckles, just like that doll you had when we were kids." It's nice to have this sisterly moment with her.

"Delilah? I loved that doll."

"What happened to that doll anyway?" I ask, leaning back against my headboard and finally relaxing.

"Danny ripped her head off."

I start laughing, and so does she, and we proceed to have

a nice conversation about her kids and Mom and our good memories with Danny. Even though we didn't have a service for our brother, I find that I'm able to bury some of my old wounds with him and my sister during one simple phone conversation.

"Well, I'd better check on Harper before I go to bed," I say.

"Good night, Indy. And please call me if you need anything, okay?"

"Thanks. Good night."

I check on Harper and then go into my old bedroom. It looks so different now. The awful folding closet doors have been replaced with two regular doors that open outward. I remember how they used to come off the tracks all the time and almost crush me as a kid.

I walk to the window and stare out into the black night sky. No one lives in the house next door right now, apparently, but I can see the lights on at Dawson's house. I wonder what he's doing right now. Is he grading papers? Talking to a woman he loves on the phone? Waiting for me to turn on a strobe light?

The thought makes me smile. I sure wish I had a strobe light right about now.

"INDY? YOU HERE?" I hear Dawson's voice call from the front door. It's Peach Valley, and locking the front door during the day just isn't done.

"In the kitchen," I call back. He walks in with a stack of papers and a smile.

"Hey."

"Hey there." He looks around the room with a goofy grin on his face as I wipe my wet hands on a dish towel. Harper is taking a nap since she missed school today. "What are you smiling about?"

"I just realized... I've never been in your house before."

"Really? Wow. I thought you had but I guess your Mom..."

"Didn't let me. Yeah. She was weird about stuff," he says. "So, anyway, I brought Harper's work she missed. Just so she has a chance to catch up this weekend if she feels better." He lays the stack on the kitchen table and looks out the back window. "Ah. The infamous swing. I remember you talking about that being your quiet place as a kid."

"Good memory," I say as I join him in looking out the window. "Actually, that's a new wooden swing from the Drager Brothers' shop on Main."

"Nice. Looks sturdy."

I smile. "Wanna try it out with me?"

He nods and shoves his hands into his jean pockets as we walk out into the backyard. It's early evening, and the air is starting to get cool, so I pull my cardigan tighter around me before sitting down.

"So this is where young Indy would hang out with her boom box, huh?"

"Yep. I remember that my friend Tabitha and I would sit here for hours listening to the weekly top forty countdown on the radio."

"And making mixed tapes?"

"Of course. We were super cool like that."

A long moment passes as we both just sit there, taking in the smoke tinged fall air, listening the crackling of the dead leaves at our feet as we push the swing ever forward.

"I came looking for you... the day you left."

"You did?" he asks, turning slightly toward me.

"My parents announced their divorce, and it was horrible, of course. I needed you, but you were gone."

I can see him start to reach for me, as if to touch my leg, but he stops himself. "Oh, Indy. I'm so sorry I wasn't there, especially since you were there for me so many times."

"It was tough. Right after that, my grandfather died and my mother just broke down."

"How is your mother?"

"She died awhile ago, after a long battle with cancer. She also had early dementia which just made things so much harder."

"I'm so sorry. I know you loved her."

"And your mother?"

"On husband number nine living in Vegas working at a doughnut shop."

I start laughing even as I try to stifle it. "Seriously?"

He smiles and shakes his head. "Yep. I haven't talked to her in many years, though. Too much drama."

"I can understand that. I don't like drama either. And your sister?"

"First, Mom put her in a home for disabled people. Then she took her out and moved her to Vegas for awhile. But then she passed away a few years ago after a battle with pneumonia. I went to the funeral, but steered clear of my mother. Some things are better left alone."

"I'm so sorry about your sister, Dawson."

We swing for a few moments in silence. "So Harper is your brother's daughter, right?"

"Yes."

"You never talked about him much."

"I wasn't allowed to. My brother was a drug addict, and my mother taught me to keep the family secrets to myself. Although, I told you more than just about anybody other than Tabitha."

He takes over the pushing as I pull my legs up and hug my knees. "You know I didn't want to leave, right?"

75

I look at him. He has the beginnings of crow's feet around his dark eyes, but it looks so good on him. "I know. How did it happen?"

"Well, after my stupendous choice of calling the fire department, my mother was livid. She wanted to be with her boyfriend at the time, so she shipped me off to some horrific place in the deep, dark forests of North Carolina. Let's just say that prison would've been a safer place in my mind."

"Oh, Dawson. I'm so sorry you had to go through that."

"Eighteen months she left me there. When I got out, I was messed up. By that time, she'd moved to Texas, so I was stuck in a totally new state that I knew nothing about. When I hit sixteen, I ran away and I've been on my own ever since."

"How did you afford college?"

"Military. I joined the Army as soon as I could and ended up with two tours in Iraq."

My heart stops. The thought of him in a war zone… Had I known at the time, it would have slayed me.

"Iraq. Wow. I… What was that like?"

His face changes, almost like he's lost any expression at all. His eyes aren't looking at me. They're looking someplace else that I can't see, to some other time.

"I don't really like to talk about it," he says softly. As a therapist, I should know better than to just blurt out a question like that. Before I can apologize, he stands up and puts his hands in his pockets again. "Listen, I gotta go. Tell Harper I hope she feels better soon, okay?"

Before I can walk him to the door, he's there and then into the house and out the front door. And I'm left to wonder what happened to my sweet Dawson in Iraq.

When did life get so damn complicated?

CHAPTER 6

I stand in front of the fig tree, staring up at the massive thing, wondering what in the world I'm going to do with it. Even when my dad would cut it to the ground and burn the stump, the stupid thing would come back stronger. Quite a metaphor for my own life.

If there's one thing my life has taught me, it's strength. Being strong after my parents' divorce was difficult. The very next morning, I remember sitting in the middle of the living room floor, playing a board game with Tabitha. I suddenly started crying, missing my father and grieving for the loss of my once perfect family.

My mother, thinking that tough love was the only love, walked through the room and told me to cut it out. She said we had to get on with life, and to stop crying. It taught me that showing emotion meant showing weakness and that vulnerability was a dangerous thing. I've spent most of my adulthood trying to shake the feeling that when good things are going on, something bad must be around the corner.

"Why are you staring at that tree?" Harper says from behind me.

"You're up. Good. You look a lot better. How do you feel?"

"Like someone ran over me with a truck. But better, I guess." She sits down on the steps, which means she's going to hang out with me for at least a bit, and that makes me happy. "So why are you always staring at that thing?"

"Well, I'm trying to figure out how to trim it without killing it or myself."

"Can't we just chop it down? It's way too big."

I laugh. "Trust me, chopping it down only makes it angry, and then it comes back stronger." I take a seat next to her. "It's called a fig tree."

"What are figs?"

I get up and look inside the tree, pulling a ripe purple hued fig off one of the branches. "Here. Taste it."

"Ew. No way! It's not even washed."

I bite off the end of the fig and smile at the sweetness of it. "When something is grown outside without chemicals, it's not as important to wash it before you eat it."

"What do they taste like?"

I pull another one from the tree. "I can't describe it. Here, you taste for yourself." She takes the fig and stares at it for a moment, but finally takes a bite.

"They look weird."

"But how does it taste?"

"Not too bad." I sit back down beside her and toss my fig stem into the bushes next to us.

"I remember when I was a kid, my Mom would have all of us out here picking figs in the evening. She would make canned preserves out of them. We had so many figs that strangers would stop and knock on our door asking if they could pick some."

"Did my Daddy pick figs too?" she asks softly.

"Of course he did! He was the tallest. Danny was the only

one who could get the top limbs, but even he had to use a ladder sometimes."

Out of the corner of my eye, I see her smile. "He never told me about the figs."

"Did he ever tell you about the motorcycle?"

She looks at me and cocks her head. "Motorcycle?"

"Come with me," I say as I walk her the short distance to the big oak tree. "See this gash?"

She runs her hand across it. "Yeah?"

"Your father made me ride a motorcycle... well, more of a dirtbike... with him when I was about eleven years old. And then he ran both of us into this tree!"

It's the first time I've heard her laugh. And I love the sound. It touches a place in my heart that I didn't even know was there.

"And out here, on this road, he and his friends would ride their dirt bikes up and down the street. They were so loud! But your Daddy could stand on one pedal with his whole body on one side of the bike and ride up that hill," I say pointing. I can see Danny in my mind, smiling and yelling at each stunt he did. It brings a smile to my face.

"Tell me more stories... about my Dad."

I take in a quick breath and smile. "Okay. Why don't we go make some breakfast and I'll tell you all about the time that he set the woods on fire behind the house."

"He did what?" she says giggling as she follows me inside.

I'M BORED. Peach Valley isn't exactly the hotbed of activity I'd hoped for. I miss counseling people. I miss just being around people.

The last couple of weeks with Harper have been a slow build, but I found that Dawson was right. Talking to her about her father has been the best course of action. It opens her up, and it shows her that I really did try to love him. I can show her that without talking bad about him. There are enough good times stored in my memory bank to give her that gift.

But we still have our moments. Moments when she misses her Dad. Moments when I resent him for doing this to me. Moments when I wish I could turn back time and try to help him. Moments when I wish I could have said a proper goodbye to Dawson and begged him to never go to war.

Sitting around the house all day is driving me stir crazy, and so I've decided to find a job. I have to use my skills. One day I can go back to Charleston, to my life there. But for now I'm stuck in Peach Valley because Harper's life is more important than mine at the moment.

My doorbell rings, which is unusual in the middle of the day, and I find a courier standing there.

"Hello, ma'am. I've got a letter delivery for you."

"Thank you," I say, signing the clipboard and then closing the door. The letter is from some attorney's office in Atlanta, but I don't recognize the name.

I sit down on my sofa and immediately feel faint when I open it. My brother's handwriting. I'd know it anywhere.

It was dated a few months before he died, probably around the time he changed his will. Ethan must not have known he had more than one attorney, which is weird for a guy who struggled to make ends meet. That alone shows me how much his daughter meant to him.

Dear Indy,

Well, my little sister, I bet you're surprised to see this letter from me. I should've written you years ago, but we both know there were hard feelings there. I know you had to protect yourself from the guy I was way back then, but I hope you know by now - by meeting Harper - that I got better. And she's the best part of me.

I don't want to die - I mean who wants to take an eternal dirt nap - but I know that things can happen and I want to make sure my baby girl is well taken care of. That's why I chose you.

Knowing you - with all your questions - you're wondering why I chose you and not Amy or someone else. I want to tell you why so you can just focus on raising my daughter:

I chose you because you ask hard questions and demand answers. My baby needs someone who will always be on her side and fight for her.

I chose you because your capacity for love has always been big. My baby needs to be loved no matter what she does.

I chose you because you're smart. My baby needs someone who will make smart decisions for her when she can't make them for herself.

I chose you because I messed up so many times, Indy, and I wanted to apologize by giving you the thing most precious to me in all the world. I have nothing else to give.

Take care of her. Maybe tell her some good things about her old Dad. Please love her, and please know that I never stopped loving you.

Danny

I crumple to the floor in a million shattered pieces, and grief sweeps over me in a way I can't describe. I miss my brother. I miss the relationship we could've had. I want to run out into the street and hunt down every drug dealer he ever came across. I want so many things right now, but what I end up doing is crying in a heap on the floor until my tear ducts run dry.

TURNS out that Peach Valley doesn't have a large job pool. I run by the school to bring Harper her forgotten lunch bag after spending the morning looking for jobs all over town.

"Hey, Indy. That for Harper?" the receptionist at the front desk asks as I walk into the school.

"Yes. She forgot it again. That girl would forget her head if it wasn't attached!"

She laughs and walks down the hall to deliver it. As I walk toward the door, I hear Dawson call out to me.

"Hey. What're you doing here?"

"Harper forgot her lunch."

"Again? Jeez, that kid."

"Got to get back to job hunting," I say, weariness all over my face.

"Job hunting?"

"Yes, but it turns out Peach Valley isn't the place to look for any jobs, especially counseling. Must be a bunch of mentally stable people living here," I say with a laugh.

I can see the wheels turning in his head. "Listen, I heard something this morning but you can't repeat it." He pulls me to the side like we're about to discuss a state secret.

"What?"

"Evelyn Calloway is taking an early retirement starting next week."

"You mean the counselor here?"

"Yes. Her husband got some bad medical news yesterday, so she's going home to take care of him full-time."

"Oh, that's very sad," I say, trying to sound humane but wanting him to get to the point because the smell of his cologne is making me want to do things that might get me arrested in a school.

"Indy, I think I can get you the job. If you want it, that is."

School counselor? I have never considered that, mainly because I don't have kids of my own. But being at the school and closer to Harper sounds like a good option. Her behavior has improved, but being visible around the school might be a great way to keep her in check.

82

"I'd definitely be interested." I wonder how Harper will feel about it, though. I definitely don't want to set our relationship back when it's just beginning.

"Let me pull some strings. I'll come by this evening, if that's okay?"

I smile. "Sure, neighbor."

HARPER PUTS her head on the kitchen table and sighs. "I don't understand it."

"Okay. Let's try it again. If Sally is one foot taller than Jeremy but six inches shorter than…"

"Can we take a break? Please?" She slaps her hand against her forehead. "My brain is going to explode."

I smile as I remember feeling the same way about those crazy word problems when I was a kid. And why is Sally so dang tall anyway?

"Yes, you can take a break. One hour and then we're back at it."

"Great! Can I go to Olivia's house? She invited me to eat dinner."

"Is Olivia's mom okay with that?"

"Yes."

"Okay. But you have to be back right at eight. Deal?"

She gives me the slightest smile and nods. "Eight."

I like they way that our relationship is growing a little each day. I can feel her starting to trust me, even starting to respect me. Baby steps, I remind myself everyday.

As I watch her walk down the hill in front of our house, I stand in the window and breathe in deeply. For once, I'm starting to feel at home and relaxed. Life is slower in Peach Valley, even though life wasn't all that fast in Charleston.

"Knock knock." Dawson is standing in the doorway holding a brown paper bag. "Chinese?"

I smell the scent of what I believe to be Mongolian Beef, which is my favorite. "How did you know I wouldn't have eaten yet?"

"I took a chance."

"Come on in," I say, waving him through the foyer.

"Where's Harper?"

"She went to eat at Olivia's house. Math was making her brain explode, apparently."

"Ahhh. Word problems?"

"Yep." He sits the bag on the kitchen table.

"I was thinking maybe we could eat outside on the patio?" For some reason my stomach fills with butterflies at the thought of sitting in the dim evening sky with Dawson, but I brush the anxiety away.

"Sure. Let me grab my sweater."

We head outside with the bag. I grab a couple of Cokes and a candle since we'll be losing all daylight within a short time.

As Dawson spreads out the food, I smile at the easiness of it all. Like we didn't have a separation of almost two decades.

"How did you know I even like Chinese food?"

"Because you told me a long time ago," he says with a smile. "Mongolian beef. Egg rolls. Sizzling rice soup." He holds up each item as he says their names.

"I was twelve. I've changed quite a bit since then," I say, pointing my hand up and down my body. He slowly scans over my body before meeting my eyes, sending chills up my spine.

"Some things never change, and loving Chinese food is one of those things." I laugh, trying to usher the blush away from my face.

"So, what's the occasion?" I ask as I sit down in the

wrought iron chair, adjusting the fluffy seat pad underneath me. He lights the candle, and I can see a smile spread across his face.

"Well, I come bearing good news, Miss Stone."

"Ms. Sanders."

"Yeah, whatever. When are you going to change that back to your cool name?"

"That's what Ethan asked me."

"Who's Ethan?"

"Never mind. Old friend from school."

"Boyfriend?" he asks, a hint of aggravation in his voice. I start laughing.

"No. He's married, first of all. He handled the paperwork for my brother and Harper."

"Oh," he says, and I swear I can see a shade of red spread across his tanned face. "Sorry."

I brush it off to avoid embarrassing either of us. "So, what's this news?" I reach across and take one of the styrofoam containers that has brown rice and Mongolian Beef.

"You got the job," he says before biting into an egg roll. "I mean if you want it."

"What? I didn't even have an interview!"

"I talked you up a little bit."

"Oh really? Does that mean you think I'm super special, Dawson Woods?" I ask playfully. He stops and leans toward me across the table.

"The most special person I've ever known." His voice is soft and gravely, and I feel paralyzed in place for a moment. He holds my gaze before smiling and taking another bite of his egg roll. "Mind if we have a little music?"

"Sure," I say, feeling more like this is a date and not a congratulatory dinner from my sexy neighbor. He pulls out his phone and plays some easy listening channel on low volume. Right now, I'd kind of rather hear rap music or death metal so it didn't feel so dang romantic out here.

"So, are you going to take the job?" he asks, taking a bite of rice.

"I'd like to know more about it before I commit, Dawson. You know, important stuff like benefits, salary, job requirements…"

He laughs. "Buzz kill."

"Ha ha. I'm an adult now. I have to think practically, especially now that I'm Harper's mother."

He smiles. "That's the first time I've heard you call yourself her mother and not her guardian or aunt."

"Baby steps."

"You're going to be a great mother, Indy. I always thought so."

I bite my egg roll and smile. "Really? And why would a twelve year old boy be thinking that? Especially one who never wanted to get married?"

"I was a deeper thinker than you thought I was."

"So, did you ever get married?" I ask, leaning back in my chair and crossing my arms. He smiles crookedly, one dimple appearing that I never noticed before.

"Nope. That hasn't changed." My stomach knots up in a way I hadn't expected. Why should I care whether he ever gets married?

"That's a pity. Marriage can be great."

"Like yours?" he says offhandedly. My face goes slack, my expression gone. "I'm sorry, Indy. I didn't meant to say that…"

"Out loud? Yeah, well, you did. And you don't know anything about my marriage, Dawson. Stay in your lane, okay?"

"Point taken," he says, holding up his hands in defeat. "So, about the job… You just need to come in tomorrow and talk to Principal Headrick. It's really a formality, though. They need someone quick, and you're definitely overqualified for the job."

"How exactly do you know so much about my qualifications anyway?"

"I Googled you."

I laugh. "Gotta love technology."

"Mr. Woods? What are you doing here?" Harper says from the back doorway.

"Oh, hi, Harper. Egg roll?" Dawson asks.

"Turns out, Mr. Woods is an old friend of mine. We knew each other when we were twelve… for a few months," I say, trying to explain our relationship.

"That's weird," she says with her nose scrunched up. "And creepy."

"How is that weird?" Dawson asks with a laugh.

She pauses for a moment. "I don't know, but it's weird."

"I thought you were eating at Olivia's?" I ask.

"I was but her little brother got sick, and I hate when people throw up so I came home."

"I can understand," Dawson says. "Have a seat. We have plenty of Chinese."

She walks to the table and looks back and forth at us as if she's trying to figure out the hardest math problem of her life. "So you knew each other a long, long time ago?"

I pile some rice and Mongolian Beef on her plate, and she immediately starts segregating the green onions to one side. "It wasn't exactly horse and buggy days, but yes we were friends back then. Just for about three months, though, because Dawson had to move."

"Where'd you move to?" she asks, putting a scoop of rice into her mouth.

"North Carolina." He takes a sip of his sweet tea and eyes me seriously as if he's looking for backup.

"So, Harper, Mr. Woods brought me some interesting news. Mrs. Calloway is retiring and the school might want to hire me as the counselor. What do you think about that?"

She freezes, fork dangling in midair, and stares at me. Her red eyelashes blink up and down slowly as her jaw drops. "You mean you'll be at my school all day long? Every single day?"

Dawson chuckles and then stifles it. "She'll be there doing her job, but you probably won't even see her unless you want to."

She finally starts moving again and takes another bite of her food. "I guess it's fine. Just don't embarrass me."

I laugh at that and we continue eating dinner, chatting about all sorts of things. It feels like a family. The only problem is, this family is highly dysfunctional and can never be a real family anyway.

The question is - why does that bother me more than it should?

CHAPTER 7

*A*fter the formalities are out of the way, I'm working at the school right alongside Dawson and Harper. As I sit at my desk, looking out the window at kids running laps during PE, I realize how much my life has changed in just a few short weeks.

I'm making strides with Harper, or at least I think so. She talks to me after school, lets me help her with homework, laughs when I tell her things about her father. The anger seems to be dissipating, and that's really all I can ask for.

My anger at him has disappeared too.

"Indy? I'm leaving for a dental appointment," the secretary at the front desk says. "Katie will be manning the desk."

"Okay. Good luck at the dentist!"

"Ugh. I hate the dentist…" she laments as she walks away.

After meeting with two parents and one very unruly child this morning, I decide to take a quick walk outside for some much needed fresh air. It's almost lunch time anyway, so my next meeting isn't until after one o'clock.

I don't see Dawson at school much, mainly because he's

on the hall furthest from me, and that's probably good because being around him leaves me with confused feelings.

I don't know what we're doing. We spend a lot of time together like this strange little family that isn't a family - eating, doing yard work, taking walks. But Dawson has always made it clear that he never wants to get married or have a family.

And why am I even thinking about this? We aren't dating. And I don't know if I ever want to get married again either.

Yep, fresh air is definitely needed.

I walk outside to a small patio that overlooks the big grassy field used for PE. I can see the kids are finishing up some kind of relay race and walking back toward the building for lunch, so maybe I can get a quiet few minutes to recharge for my afternoon schedule.

"Indy Stone?" I hear a male voice say from in front of me. I've been looking down at my phone, responding to former clients in Charleston. When I look up, I see a very handsome man, but the sunlight behind his golden locks is blinding me enough that I don't recognize him. I slide my sunglasses down from my head and immediately make the connection.

"Kent Akers?" My eyes are wide when I see who it is. I had never expected to see my junior prom date standing in front of me. Kent's family had moved to Germany the summer before our senior year, thus breaking up our budding romance.

He steps forward and draws me into a warm embrace, which startles me at first and then I remember that most people are normal and enjoy hugs. I'm just a little skittish, but it only takes a moment to welcome the touch of a good looking man.

"What are you doing here?" he asks with a bright smile, stepping under the overhang.

"I work here now. I replaced Mrs. Calloway as the counselor."

"Wow. Small world, huh?"

"When did you move back to Peach Valley?" We both sit down across from each other at the picnic table.

"Oh, ages ago. I've been the PE teacher here for about eight years now. And how did you end up here?"

"Just moved back to take care of my niece after my brother died. I was a therapist in Charleston."

"Married?" he asks, a gleam in his eye.

"Not anymore, no."

Kent is as good looking as ever. I can imagine that the teachers here are probably fawning over him daily with his thick, wavy blond hair and crystal clear blue eyes. Those were two of the things that drew me to him back in high school. And now he's a real man with a muscular build to prove it.

As the quarterback of our football team, every girl wanted to be with Kent Akers. He'd had his pick of prom dates, and for some reason he'd chosen to ask me. At the time, I thought maybe it was a prank gone wrong, but we'd had a fabulous time.

"Gosh, it's so good to see you, Indy. Maybe we can get together some time, for dinner?"

My stomach clenches up for reasons I can't explain. "Sure. Soon. I'm just really busy trying to get acclimated right now..."

Sensing my tension, he smiles easily. "Of course. Well, if there's anything I can do to help you get... acclimated... let me know, okay?" I swear, he'd be perfect for toothpaste commercials or the cover of an LL Bean catalog.

"Coach Akers? I skinned my knee," a little boy says from around the corner of the building.

"Eli, you were supposed to be inside already. Jeez... I'll see you later, Indy," he says, squeezing my shoulder as he stands and jogs off to the little boy who is acting as though his entire leg is about to fall off.

"Already impressing the men around here, I see," a voice says from the corner of the building. Dawson is leaning against the brick, his arms crossed.

"What?" He walks over to me lazily and takes the spot that Kent was occupying moments before. Suddenly, I feel like I'm on one of those speed dating TV shows.

"Kent Akers? Come on."

"Excuse me?"

"He's the epitome of a pretty boy, Indy. All hat and no cattle. Surely you can't be interested in him?"

I laugh. "And what if I was?"

"Well, I just thought more of you than that. I mean he's pretty shallow, don't you think?"

"Why do I sense a competition here, Dawson?" I'm finding immense amounts of humor in his apparent jealous streak as I watch his jaw tense and start to palpitate.

"No competition. You can do what you want. But don't you think it's weird that this guy barely knows you…"

"He was my prom date."

He stops speaking and his face goes blank for a moment. "Your prom date?"

I lean across the table and smile. "Yes. He knows more of me than you do, Mr. Woods." His mouth drops open a little bit as I stand and walk to the door. "Have a good day."

I wish I could turn around and see his face, but it would ruin the moment for me. I'm far too old to play games, but I have to admit that was kind of fun. Maybe being around kids is bringing out my playful side. Or my petty one.

HARPER RUNS around the house gathering things as she goes. "Do you have your toothbrush?"

"Yes…." she groans back at me from the end of the hall.

"And what about your shampoo?"

"Yes…."

"Don't forget an extra pair of underwear…"

"Aunt Indy! I know!" she yells back from her bedroom. That's the first time she's called me anything. Aunt Indy. I'm okay with that.

A last minute trip to Olivia's family's cabin in the mountains is a welcome surprise for Harper. I wondered if I should let her go. Would Danny have allowed it? I don't know. But we need a little space from each other, and she's doing so well in school that I decide to give her some room.

She comes barreling down the hall with her backpack and pillow, a smile on her face. "I've got everything I own."

"Oh! What about your vitamins?" I say, looking toward the kitchen cabinet where we keep such things.

"It's fine. My body won't break down over one weekend," she says as she runs toward the front door. Olivia's parents' car pulls into the driveway just as we make it to the foyer.

"Bye!" she calls over her shoulder as she runs to their car and starts loading her bags into the trunk. I wave at the back of her head and start walking back inside, but she surprises me when she runs back and gives me a quick hug without looking at me. I say nothing and hug her back, but she's gone before I can really feel the moment.

It's progress.

I SIT on the sofa in my now quiet house and take in a deep breath. I miss her, which is not something I expected. It's

Friday night, and I could easily turn on the TV and veg out for the night, but I'm feeling antsy. I want to do something.

As I'm walking to the kitchen, debating what to do with my evening and considering a glass of wine, I hear a knock at my front door. When I open it, no one is there. Just as I'm about to slam it shut and complain about "kids these days" like an old person, I notice a brown box at the edge of the steps with a big red bow on it. I look around and see no one.

My first instinct is to call the bomb squad, but I realize I'm in Peach Valley where the likelihood that someone is trying to kill me is pretty small. So I scoop up the box and head back inside, locking the front door behind me.

There's no name on the box, so I assume it's for me since I do own the place. I pull off the one piece of clear tape that's holding the box together and the flaps pop open to reveal my gift inside. A strobe light.

I immediately smile. I know exactly who this is from. There's also a note.

Dear Indy,

I'm sorry I acted like an ass about Kent. I miss seeing you dance. Waiting at my window.

- Dawson

All of the sudden, I'm transported back to being twelve years old, and butterflies are darting around my empty stomach. Deciding that I need a little liquid courage, I pour a glass of wine and take a sip. I'm not a regular drinker - especially given my family history - but I haven't danced in years. I need a little something to take the edge off.

A part of me is screaming, "You're an adult! Don't dance in the window. Be serious!" The other part is begging me to let go and have some fun. The second part wins.

I pull the strobe light out of the box and walk to my old bedroom. As I search my phone for the right dance music, I imagine Dawson sitting in his window, hands under his chin as he waits for the show.

I find the 80's channel on my satellite radio app and turn up the volume. Then I plug in the strobe light and start its flashing lights before turning off my bedroom light.

The only thing left is opening the blinds. I slowly raise them up and can just see the silhouette of Dawson sitting in his window. The sight makes me smile more than I thought it would.

Taking another sip of my wine, I start moving to a Cyndi Lauper song. Within minutes, I'm my twelve year old self again, arms flailing. My dancing was never sexy, but was always entertaining. Sometimes I'd even invite my girlfriends over to spend the night and join me in my dance party.

After three songs, I poke my head up to see if Dawson is still there. He's not. Maybe the show wasn't as good as he remembered. As I'm staring out into the dark night, he taps on my window and scares me to death.

"Dawson! You almost gave me a heart attack!" I say as I raise the window up. "Why are you out here?"

"I wanted a closer look. My eyes aren't what they used to be," he says with a smile.

"Old age getting you?" I respond sarcastically. He leans against the tree outside my window. "I thought maybe my show wasn't as good as you'd remembered."

"Oh, it was better than I remembered. You've got skills, Indy." I know he's being funny, but the way he says it sounds totally serious.

"Don't you have anything better to do with your Friday night?" I ask as I sit on the edge of my windowsill.

"I can't remember a Friday night I've enjoyed more than this one." Again, he doesn't crack a smile.

"Well, maybe we need to find you a hobby." I always make

jokes when things get serious. It's a coping mechanism that has served me well my whole life.

"Stop joking around, Indy," he says, walking closer until his face is mere inches away. "You always joke when you're nervous."

How does he remember that? "Why would I be nervous?" I am nervous, but I can't really pinpoint why.

He finally smiles. "I don't know, but I'm nervous too."

"Why are you nervous?" I ask, swinging my legs outside of the window and wondering where the screens went that we had on the house when I was a kid. I hold on to the molding around the inside of the window.

"I guess because I can't believe I'm here."

"Where? In Peach Valley?"

"No. With you again. I never thought this would happen. I hoped it would, but I thought I might never see you again." He leans back against the tree again a few feet away. "Can I ask you something?"

"Sure…"

"Did you ever think about me? I mean all these years later?"

I cock my head to the side and pretend to be thinking. Then I decide to be honest. "Yes. All the time."

His smile beams so much that I can see it in the dark. "Same here."

"You were only in my life for a short time, Dawson. But it was a hard time, and I really appreciated our friendship. It helped me get through a lot, even if you didn't know it."

He sighs and looks up at the clear sky. "Andromeda"

"What?"

He points up at the sky. "The constellation. You can only see her during the fall."

I laugh. "I didn't know you were a big constellation expert."

He smiles. "When I was a kid, I had a lot of alone time. One of the step dads bought me a book about stars, and I used to stare out my window and try to name them. Andromeda is my favorite."

"Why?"

"The constellation is named for Andromeda, the daughter of Cassiopeia. It's from a Greek myth. Anyway, as the myth goes, she was chained to a rock to be eaten by a sea monster."

"That sounds… violent."

"Cassiopeia made the mistake of bragging that Andromeda was prettier than this other chick. Because of that, Poseidon punished Cassiopeia by having these sea monsters attack Ethiopia. But Andromeda's father found out that he could save them by sacrificing his daughter, so he chained her to a rock."

"Nice father."

"Yeah. Then along comes the hero of the story - Perseus. He saves Andromeda and then they got married. They say that Athena then put Andromeda in the sky after her death to honor her." He stares upward. "Want to see her?"

"Okay," I say, as I gingerly try to jump down from the window. I start to slip just as Dawson catches me before I hit the ground. My body slides against his as he holds me tightly with his arms around my waist.

We stand there for a moment until I shuffle my feet. "Got it. Sorry about that."

He lets go and looks back up at the sky. "Okay, see that bright star right there above the tree?"

I look up but I truly have no idea what he's referring to. "No. Sorry."

He steps behind me and puts his arms around my waist again. I feel my legs start to buckle. What is wrong with me? He leans down and puts his mouth next to my ear.

"Okay, now look up between those two branches. See that really bright star?"

"Mhmm…" I say, trying to keep my composure.

"That's the brightest star in Andromeda. It's ninety-seven light years from Earth…"

He goes on and on, but I can't hear a word he's saying. All I feel are his strong arms around my waist and his warm breath against my ear. His cologne is invading every one of my senses, and the stubble on his jaw is tickling my own jawline. I've never wanted to turn around and kiss someone so much in my life.

When he's finished explaining, he steps back. "Cool, huh?"

"Yes. Cool," I say, feeling like a teenager even using that word. "I guess I'd better get back inside."

"Is Harper here?"

"No, she went on a weekend trip with Olivia's family."

He smiles. "Mind if I come in? I'm supremely bored at my house. We could order a pizza."

"Okay. Let me just climb back through my window and unlock the front door." I turn and realize my window is way too high to go back into it from his angle. But before I can say anything, I feel Dawson lifting me up, one hand on my butt. *His hand is on my butt.* I pull myself through the window and walk back to the front door to open it for him, but I stop for a moment to take a deep breath because *his hand was just on my butt.*

I call and order the pizza, and they're going to be at least forty-five minutes because it's Friday night and people like pizza in Peach Valley, apparently.

"Want to sit on the patio?"

"Nope. But I'll sit on that nifty swing you have," he says with a chuckle. We walk out to the swing and sit down. "Do you know why I like the Andromeda constellation the most?"

Great. We're back on constellations again. "No. Why?"

"The story. I feel like I'm Andromeda."

I giggle. "You're the female in the story?"

He nudges me with his shoulder. "Think about it. My mother wasn't exactly… well, motherly. She basically put me out there as a sacrifice. She didn't care what happened to me, Indy."

"I have to believe she loved you in her own completely dysfunctional way. But yes, she hung you out to dry most of the time."

"You were Perseus."

"What?"

"My hero."

"But I didn't save you, Dawson. I was just a kid down the street you hung out with for a few weeks," I say softly.

"You saved me in more ways than you know, Indy."

"I don't understand," I say, turning slightly to face him. He turns to face me too. "How exactly did I save you?"

"The day you walked by and sneezed… I was going to kill myself that day, Indy. I had a bottle of my mom's pills in my hand when I saw you. I had never seen a girl so pretty."

My heart pounds against my chest. A sick feeling washes across my whole body as I think of him sitting there in his room with death only moments away.

"I had no idea, Dawson. But you seemed so… okay…"

"Years of practice."

"But why did me walking by matter to you?"

"Something about you. Your face. Your laugh. Your wit. When I met you, I knew there was hope out there, even in my twelve year old mind. I knew I had to see you again, so I put the pills back in my mother's bathroom. And it was the hope of someday finding you again that kept me going, even in Iraq."

"I don't know what to say."

"Don't say anything," he says, putting his index finger over my lips. "I just want to say thank you."

We sit there silent for a moment before he removes his finger and sits back.

"So, tell me about your husband."

"Ex husband," I correct quickly.

"Right. Tell me about that moron," he responds, which elicits a laugh from me.

"Well, there's not much to say. Fell in love in college. He was my professor."

"What?" he chokes out.

"We didn't start dating until the semester after I was in his abnormal psychology class," I say quickly, as if that makes it better.

"Ah, the irony of the class title."

"Funny. Anyway, David was an amazing teacher. He's only four years older than me, but he just seemed so wise at the time. So we dated for about a year and then got married on a whim while we were on vacation in Atlantic City."

"No big wedding?"

"Nope."

"But you wanted a big wedding, right?"

"You remember that?"

"Yes. I remember that you told me you wanted the beautiful church with the flowing white gown and a big reception with dancing."

"Wow. I can't believe the guy who never wants to get married remembers that," I say with a smile. "David didn't want a big wedding, so we didn't have one."

"Seems to me that a man who's in love would give his future wife the wedding of her dreams." He says it softly, not like he's poking fun at me but just stating a fact.

"We were married for twelve years, but then one day he met a new woman. One of his students. Again."

I can see the twitch in Dawson's jaw as I tell him the story. "He cheated on you?"

"Yes."

"What a freaking idiot. Who cheats on you, Indy? I mean seriously…" He's mumbling more than he's talking to me.

"I'm nothing special, Dawson. It happens to women - and men - all the time."

He slides closer and puts his hand on my cheek. "You are special, Indy Stone. And any man who can't see that deserves to be tossed off the nearest cliff."

"Yeah, well, we don't have cliffs around here," I whisper, a heat coming over my face and then running down my body as I feel his hand on my cheek.

He stares into my eyes, and we freeze in place, only the sound of our breathing breaking through the moment. I feel transported back in time, sitting in a fig tree about to be kissed for the first time.

"Somebody order a pizza?" I hear the delivery guy say over the chain link fence.

"Yes, we did," I call back as I slip from under Dawson's hand and start walking to the side gate. I can hear Dawson's footsteps behind me.

"*Now* they're early…" he mumbles, referencing how late the pizza delivery companies usually are around here. I giggle to myself, probably confusing the poor teenage boy. "I've got it." Dawson pulls out his wallet and settles up with the boy before following me to the picnic table with the pizza box.

"I'll go grab some drinks," I say as I go back into the house to calm myself down. I can't kiss Dawson again. It almost ruined me at twelve years old, and now I'm decades wiser. Kissing a man, for me at least, leads to feelings that won't work with Dawson. He never wants to get married, and even though my last marriage ended in divorce, I don't want to rule out getting married again. I can't start something that Dawson can't finish.

I go back outside with some paper plates, napkins and canned drinks. Dawson has the pizza box open when I return, his face leaned in as he inhales the strong aroma.

"Nothing like Dominic's Pizza," he says.

"Yeah. I've missed this. When I was a teenager, we would always order from there. My friend, Tabitha, and I would save our pennies and literally count out nine-hundred of them when the poor delivery guy would come," I say with a laugh as I take one of the gooey slices of pepperoni pizza and flop it onto my flimsy plate.

"I bet he loved that!"

"Yeah, we were idiots back then."

"Sorry I missed knowing you as a teenager. I bet you were popular." He takes a bite of his pizza and grins.

"I guess maybe a little. I mean I wasn't cheerleader popular, but I did okay."

"And that's when you met Kent Akers, huh?"

"How did I know you were going to ask about that?" I say with a smile. "Yes, Kent was very popular. For some reason, he took a liking to me in our junior year and asked me to the prom."

"And you said he knew a lot more of you than I did…"

"I was being funny."

"Doubtful. Exactly what parts of you did he get to know on prom night, Indy Stone?" I think he's playing with me, but his eyes are boring a hole through my own as he looks at me.

"I was a good girl, Dawson."

"What exactly does that mean?"

I leaned over. "Even though it's none of your business, I was a virgin when I got married to David."

I can see him swallow hard and then he clears his throat. "Really?"

"Yep. Boring good girl here." I take another bite of my pizza.

"That's not boring, Indy. I bet David thought it was fantastic. That's a gift for a man." He winks at me.

"Can we talk about something else?" I ask as my face flushes.

"Of course. We have lots to catch up on," he says. "And the night is still young!"

And I have no idea where this night is going.

CHAPTER 8

*I*t's so quiet out here. Peach Valley seems like the quietest place on Earth tonight. I haven't heard a car go by on the road behind my house for at least half an hour, and Dawson hasn't said anything for the last few minutes, seemingly content to just lie here beside me under the stars.

After eating pizza and chatting about the last couple of decades, minus his military service, we decided to lay out a blanket in the backyard and stare up at the stars. There are a couple of feet between us, just for safety.

"Why didn't you have kids with your ex?" he asks.

"He couldn't. Low sperm motility."

"Figures."

"Dawson, you're awful!" I say, smacking him on the arm.

"Still, there's medical technology that could have made it happen, right? Or adoption?"

I sigh. "Yeah. I suppose so. It just never felt like the right time. And then our time as a couple was up."

"And you ended up with a daughter anyway," he says.

"Yes, I certainly did. And she's a handful."

"Okay, your turn," he says. We've been taking turns asking each other questions for the last hour.

"The most serious relationship you've had as an adult?"

"Wow. That's a deep question."

"Too many to choose from?" I ask with a giggle.

"Her name was Serena. We were in Iraq together on my second tour."

"Oh." I don't know what to say next because I don't want to trigger him again. "How serious was it?"

"We were making plans to get a place together after our tour was over."

"What happened?"

He's silent for a moment. "She was killed by a roadside bomb."

I can't breathe. I have no idea what to say. "Oh, Dawson. I'm so sorry…" I roll onto my side and prop up on my elbow. He turns his head and looks at me.

"It's one of the reasons I can't talk about my time at war. It's just very painful."

Instinctively, I scoot over and lay my head on his shoulder and he puts his arm around me. It's not a sexual move, but one of two people who have been through some stuff in their lives and just want to comfort each other. I wish there was something I could do to take away his pain, his memories of that time.

"Tell me about Serena."

He takes in a deep breath. "She was funny. Reminded me a lot of your humor. And she had thick dark hair. Her mother was Italian and her father was Greek, so she would joke about needing a serious waxing when she got back stateside."

I giggle. "She sounds like she had a great sense of humor."

"She did. And she was an amazing artist. She sketched a

lot while we were there, you know, in our down time. I still have a lot of those sketches."

"I'd love to see them sometime."

He pauses for a moment. "I'm sorry I ran out on you the other day... when you asked about Iraq. It's just hard to talk about, but it felt good to talk about it tonight. I think I needed that," he says, pressing his lips to the top of my head. "You always seem to know what I need, Indy Stone."

"Are you ever going to stop calling me by my maiden name?" I smile and poke him in the chest with my index finger.

"I still think of you as a maiden. Why keep that idiot's last name when it's so not as cool as your maiden name?"

I think for a moment. There really isn't a reason to keep my married name. I don't feel like Indy Sanders. I feel like Indy Stone, especially with Dawson around.

"You know what? You're right. I'm going to ask Ethan to help me change it back."

He grins broadly and pulls me closer. "Good."

We lay there, wrapped up in each other, and I don't know what to think. I can't do this. I can't fall for Dawson Woods. He can't offer me a future because of his own past. And I can't promise to not want a future with him... with someone. I still believe in true love and happy endings and soul mates. All the stuff that he apparently doesn't believe in.

And I have to be there for Harper. I can't be all lovesick over a person I only knew for less than three months when I was a kid.

Yet here I am, my head on his shoulder, his arm around me, his lips pressed into my hair - and I don't want to move. Much like the moment in the fig tree when we were kids, I just want to stay here forever.

"Your turn," I say softly.

"Biggest regret in your life?"

"I don't really believe in regrets. I think that all situations and decisions lead you to where you are in life, and I'm happy where I am right now."

"You're happy in Peach Valley... or you're happy right here in my arms?" he asks, his voice deeper and sexier. I don't dare to move.

"Both." I hear him suck in a ragged breath, and I wonder if he can feel my heart pounding against my chest. It sounds like a jackhammer in my own ears.

I feel his arm tighten around me as his other arm comes around to meet it. He holds me closer than I thought possible, causing me to have to swing my leg over him. Still, he makes no move to kiss me or anything else. We're just wrapped up together like two people who have missed each other and need some time to just "be".

"I do have one regret," I finally say, my cheek pressed against his chest.

"What's what?"

"Not fighting your mother harder when she told me she shipped you off. I wish we hadn't lost so many years..." I don't know why I'm saying this. I'm only going to hurt myself in the end by admitting that I've missed him. Needed him. Wanted him.

He pulls his arms apart and leans back so he can look me in the eye. "Indy, you were a kid. There was nothing you could have done."

"I know," I say, propping up onto one elbow and looking at him. "But I never forgot you. I never stopped hoping that we'd cross paths one day. And I never stopped worrying about you."

He clears his throat and looks at me, his eyes soft and hooded. "I know it's not the fig tree and we're not twelve, but I can't stop myself." Before I can understand what he means, his hand slides up one side of my jaw onto my cheek and he leans in, pressing his lips softly to mine. Only this time, his tongue slips into my mouth softly, dancing with my own.

I hear a small moan escape him as if he's been walking through a desert for weeks without water and I'm a full canteen of it. He slides closer as our kiss intensifies, his hand now running through my hair, hanging on for dear life.

I can't even catch my breath, but I think it's because I'm holding it in, fearful that if I breathe out my nose, he'll stop and I'll never fill the void.

But suddenly he does stop and presses his forehead to mine. "Sorry. I felt like I might just pass out for a second," he says with a nervous laugh.

I laugh too and hang my head. "Yeah, I know what you mean."

He finally looks up, his hand still caressing my cheek and smiles. "Was that okay? I mean, that I kissed you?"

I want to say no. I *should* say no. "It was more than okay."

He smiles and then pulls me close again, my head on his chest. "I never forgot that kiss, Indy."

"In the fig tree?"

"Yes. It was the standard by which all future kisses were measured."

"Um, I was twelve and not a very good kisser, Dawson."

"Literally, there was never any other kiss that could compare."

"How is that even possible?" I ask with a giggle.

"Because you were the first person in my life who accepted me for who I was, warts and all. I knew that was a goodbye kiss. I had to tell you everything I wanted to but didn't know how to say as a young kid, but do it through one kiss. I swear, I wanted time to stop. I wanted to run away and take you with me, Indy."

I hug him tighter and sigh. And that's how we apparently fall asleep.

The next memory I have is of the sun coming up over the trees. I can hear birds chirping, cars zipping down the road. I reach over, but feel that Dawson is no longer there. Maybe I dreamed the whole thing.

"Good morning, sleepy head." I strain to open my eyes in the newly risen sun, and I can see his silhouette standing above me with his hand stretched out. "Come on. I made us breakfast."

It's weird to know him as an adult. Twelve year old Dawson didn't cook, at least not that I knew of. I take his hand and he hoists me up, leading me into the house.

I can immediately smell the aroma of coffee and bacon, and there's a sweet tinge of syrup in the air too. He's made my plate already, so I sit down and survey what I'm about to eat.

As expected, there's coffee and bacon, but also the thickest homemade blueberry pancakes I've ever seen.

"Where did you learn to cook like this?" I ask as I take a big whiff of the food.

"The military taught me a lot of things," he says, sitting down with his own plate.

"How to make pancakes like this?"

"No. Actually, that was from watching cooking shows on TV," he admits with a chuckle. "I'm a little addicted to the Food Network."

"Well, everything looks amazing."

"Yes, it does," he says, cutting his eyes up at me and smiling. I blush and don't try to hide it. "So when is Harper coming home?"

"Tomorrow afternoon. I hope she's doing okay."

"I'm sure she is. What are you two doing for Thanksgiving?"

It dawns on me in that moment that Thanksgiving is just two weeks away. I totally forgot about it, and I haven't started Christmas shopping yet either. Now that I'm someone's mother, I guess I need to get better at that kind of stuff.

"No plans yet, but I guess I should figure that out so Harper can have a good Thanksgiving."

"Well, I was thinking maybe you guys could spend it with me?"

"Don't you have plans already?" I ask as I take a bite of the pancake and almost melt into my chair it's so good.

"No plans. We're kind of in the same boat with our family situations, Indy." He sips his coffee and looks at me.

"True. What did you have in mind?"

"Well, I thought maybe you and I could cook together."

I shift uncomfortably in my seat. He's acting like we're some kind of part-time family, and the last thing I want to do is confuse Harper. She's already in the middle of a very difficult transition, and she likes Dawson as her teacher. I don't want to blur any lines that might hurt her all over again.

"Dawson, I don't think that would be a good idea." I don't look at him, but take a sip of my own coffee instead.

"What? Why?" He seems genuinely confused.

"Look, I loved spending time with you last night, but that can't happen again. I have Harper to consider now. And we're not kids anymore."

"Indy, I felt something last night. Surely you can't deny that you did too."

"I can't deny that, no. But we both know that we want two different things. Harper is having a hard enough time without me adding you to the mix."

He puts down his fork and sighs as he runs his hands through his hair. "Is this about the marriage thing?"

"Partly. And I know that's ridiculous. We're not even dating each other, so marriage isn't something that's even on the horizon. But why start something that we can't finish?"

"And marriage is the only way to finish?"

"I still believe in marriage, Dawson. I believe in happy endings and soul mates and all of that stuff. Even though I've had one failed marriage, I know it can be good. I know it can last forever."

"But why do you need a piece of paper to make something last forever?"

"Why does a piece of paper mean it won't last forever to you?"

We're at a stalemate, and it's so stupid. He picks up his plate and dumps the rest of his food in the trashcan. After rinsing his plate and putting it in the dishwasher, he walks back over to the table.

"I had a good time last night, Indy." Without another word, he walks out the front door and leaves me sitting there confused.

I sit across from a young girl and her mother. The girl, Anise, has been acting up in her class. Her mother, a harried and exhausted woman with six kids, sits there with tears in her eyes.

"Mrs. Langley, this is an issue we can fix. I'm sure of it. What I'd like to do is have Anise meet with me once a week just to check in and see where we might be having problems. You can set that up with my secretary."

"Thank you, Miss Stone," she says, reminding me of how glad I am that Ethan got my name change expedited.

After the mother/daughter pair leave my office, I dig my small lunch bag out of my drawer and sink my teeth into the large apple I've been dreaming about all day. I close my eyes and take a moment to just enjoy it without interruption.

"That must be one good apple from the look on your

face." I open my eyes to find Kent standing there smiling. I'm so embarrassed.

"What can I say? I like apples," I say with a laugh. Eating an apple is not sexy, especially with a thin stream of juice running down my chin. I quickly use my napkin to wipe it away and put the apple bag in the bag to finish later. "What's up?"

He sits down on the edge of my desk and crosses his arms. "I want to invite you and Harper to Thanksgiving at my house."

My throat closes up. Dawson has already invited me, and I declined. And now he hasn't spoken to me in several days.

"I can't. But thank you for asking." I stand up and pretend to file something across the room. Kent stands up and turns my direction.

"Is this about Dawson Woods?"

Again, I can't breathe for a second. How would he know that?

"No, of course not. Dawson's an old friend from my neighborhood."

"Just friends?"

"Yep," I say, continuing to re-file things that I don't even file normally.

"Then why can't you come? Listen, I do this every year for a few teachers who don't have family. Why spend Thanksgiving alone?"

"I'm not alone. I have Harper."

"Indy, don't you think it'd be good for her to have a bigger Thanksgiving than just you and her?"

He's right, and I freaking hate it.

I turn around. "How many people are we talking?"

He counts on his hand. "Probably about ten including the two of you."

That seems innocent enough. And it's not like I don't

know Kent. Harper needs a normal family Thanksgiving, and this is as close as we're going to get.

"Okay. That sounds good. Just leave me some details on my desk sometime this week."

He smiles broadly. "Great! I'm so glad you guys will be there."

"What can I bring?"

"Just that beautiful smile," he says, matching it with his own smile, before he walks out of my office.

Peach Valley is a complicated place.

"So we're going to Mr. Akers' house for Thanksgiving?" Harper asks me, looking at me like I've completely lost my mind.

"Yes. He invited us, and I thought it'd be a nice change of pace. Plus, there will be other teachers there with no place else to go." I wipe down the kitchen counter and watch her slump into one of the kitchen chairs.

"Let me get this straight. I'm spending my Thanksgiving with a bunch of rejects who have no family that want them at their own tables?"

"You have a way with words, Harper." I struggle not to laugh at her interpretation.

"Come on Aunt Indy… It's a holiday! I don't want to spend it with a bunch of teachers, and definitely not at Mr. Akers' house."

I stop and look at her, my hand on my hip. "What do you have against Mr. Akers? He was my prom date."

"First of all, gross. Second of all, he's so… shiny and cheesy."

I giggle. "Shiny and cheesy? What does that even mean?"

"He's like one of those Ken dolls that my Dad would never buy me because he said his 'junk' didn't look right."

I cover my mouth and burst out laughing because I can just see my brother saying something like that. "Harper!"

"Well, it's true. Have you looked between a Ken doll's legs?"

"Don't talk about stuff like that."

"I'm not a baby," she says dryly. "Anyway, Mr. Akers is just too perfect."

I walk over to her. "Harper, we're going. It would be rude to cancel. Now, go get started on your homework."

She rolls her eyes - something we need to work on but I'm choosing my battles - and goes to her room. I hear my brother's voice in my head talking about Ken's "junk" again and it makes me laugh once more.

Just then, my doorbell rings. I toss the dishcloth on the counter and walk to the door expecting to see some kid selling magazines or cookies. Instead, I see Tabitha standing in front of me all grown up.

"On my gosh! Tabby!" I squeal so loudly that I can hear Harper come running from her room.

"Indy!" Tabitha says, dropping her backpack and hugging me tightly. She looks just the same, only an older version. Her hair is still glossy black and just past her shoulders. Her makeup is thicker than it was when we were teenagers, and she's a little curvier than I remember, but otherwise she's Tabitha through and through.

"Come in! I can't believe you're here!"

Tabitha walks into the foyer and puts her bag on a chair.

"I can't believe you're back in this house again," she says with a loud laugh. Tabitha has always been loud and outgoing, which was a good balance for me when we were kids. I was much more serious and quiet.

"Tabby, this is my niece, Harper," I say, trying not to

stutter and assume I can call her my daughter now. We're just not there yet. Tabitha smiles and shakes Harper's hand.

"You're simply gorgeous!" Harper grins, her cheeks turning rosy.

"Thanks."

"Tabby and I were best friends when we were kids," I explain.

"Still are, I hope," Tabitha corrected, chucking me in the shoulder.

"Of course. We have a lot of catching up to do, though. Should I start a pot of coffee?"

"Absolutely. And I hope you don't mind me crashing on your sofa for a night?" Leave it to Tabitha to just drop in unannounced, bag in hand, and assume she can stay. She has always flown by the seat of her pants.

"You know you're always welcome!"

"Can I go to Olivia's? We want to watch a scary movie."

I purse my lips and eye her carefully. "As long as it's nothing too gory."

"Oh, come on, Indy. We watched some gory movies in our time..."

"You're not helping," I mumble to Tabby. She laughs, and suddenly Peach Valley feels like home again.

"Okay, let me get this straight. The love of your life, Dawson Woods, not only lives back in his old house but you kissed him again the other night?"

"Shh. You're still the loudest person I know!" I look around the backyard, as if someone might be listening to our conversation. And for all I know, Dawson could be crouching in the bushes - which would make him a weirdo anyway.

"Well, what are you going to do? You know y'all are old enough to finally 'do the deed' if you want," she says, taking a sip of her coffee and batting her eyelashes at me.

"Very funny. Look, nothing has changed. I just had a momentary lapse of judgement. But Dawson doesn't want the same future I do, and I have Harper to think about now."

"Still so practical," she says, finishing off one cup of coffee before pouring another.

"Maybe so, but I can't risk Harper getting hurt again."

"Are you sure you aren't talking about yourself?" Tabitha has always been able to cut right through the crap.

"So, tell me about your recent life adventures..." I pour myself a second cup and smile, unwilling to argue with her.

"Well, most recently I was in Costa Rica for about four months. Beautiful place! Next, I'll be backpacking through the Blue Ridge Mountains for a few weeks with a couple of friends."

"Still a free spirit, I see."

"Always will be. Life's short, Indy. You should know that. Why waste time doing stuff that doesn't wake you up with a smile everyday?"

I can see her point, but I have no idea how to implement that in my own life right now. Instead, I feel more responsibility than I've ever felt.

"True."

"Or with hot, sexy teachers who can also wake you up with a smile," she says grinning before I kick her under the table and shake my head.

CHAPTER 9

*J*t has been several days since I've seen Dawson, and it's bothering me more than I care to admit. He's obviously upset with me, and I'm sure he's found out by now that I'll be spending Thanksgiving at Kent's house.

And I think I might have made a mistake.

I have a tendency to overthink things. It's a self protection mechanism from my childhood. I have a need to take care of things before they get me. I'm always trying to fix problems before they even become problems.

But still I know that my feelings for Dawson will only continue to grow the more time I spend around him, especially alone. And spending Thanksgiving like a little happy family would only have played into the twisted fantasy I have rolling around in my brain - the one where I install a real white picket fence in the front yard, slap on an apron and wait for Dawson to sweep me off my feet every night after work before kissing my new daughter on the forehead as we stand in her doorway watching her drift off to sleep.

Yeah, I'm sick in the head.

So, we're going to Kent's today.

Tabitha is still here, even after only planning to stay a day or two. We've had so much fun catching up that I don't want her to leave anytime soon. And I think Harper is starting to love her like I do. It's hard not to love Tabitha. She's so free spirited and open to any adventure. She's so unlike me.

"Okay, I've got the rolls and the jug of sweet tea. Harper, can you carry the pecan pie?" I say as she stares down at her phone playing some game.

"Yeah…" she mumbles as she flips her finger back and forth and remains motionless. I walk back to her and bump her foot with mine. "Put the phone in your pocket, kiddo."

She sighs and slips it into her pocket before taking the pie from the counter and walking out the front door.

"She's still not a fan of going, huh?" Tabby asks as she puts on her sweater.

"Not at all. She doesn't like Kent."

"Well, can you blame her?"

"What? He's an okay guy," I say, trying not to make eye contact with her because I know she can see right through me.

"Oh, please, Indy. You know he's shiny and cheesy…"

I laugh. "Okay, you need to stop having conversations with Harper!"

As WE PULL up in front of Kent's house, I'm taken aback by how big it is. A four-sided brick two story, it's situated in the ritziest neighborhood in Peach Valley. I wonder how he afforded this house on a teacher's paycheck.

"Wow," Harper breathes out as we pull in the driveway.

"Wow is right," Tabitha echoes. "This place is like a mansion."

I've seen big houses in Charleston, but this one looks and

feels so out of place in Peach Valley. It's bigger than anything else in the neighborhood and sits on a huge lot surrounded by a white picket fence.

"Happy Thanksgiving!" Kent says with his big toothy grin as I open my car door. He's standing there, wearing a maroon wool sweater over a white collared shirt and looks like he literally just jumped off the front of a clothing catalog. I imagine him sitting beside a roaring fire with a red Irish Setter curled up beside him while he sips a high-class coffee drink and thinks about his stock portfolio.

"Happy Thanksgiving," I say as I give him a quick hug. It's one of those "church hugs" that keeps my breasts from making contact. I don't even make eye contact because I don't want to give him the wrong impression about our reconnection.

"Happy Thanksgiving, Indy. I'm so glad you could come," he says with a smile as he holds onto my hands that he's captured in mid-air somehow.

I clear my throat and force another smile as I pull my hands back down by my sides. "Yes. Well… This is my niece, Harper." I point behind me, unaware that Harper has high-tailed it from the car toward the house. And Tabitha seems to have abandoned me as well.

Kent laughs and cocks his head to the side. "Yeah. I know Harper. Remember? I'm a teacher at her school? Where you also work?"

I feel like a complete idiot now.

"Sorry. My brain isn't firing on all cylinders today, apparently."

"It's fine, Indy. Like I said, I'm just glad you came."

I can't help but like Kent. He's always been charming and good looking. He's always known just what to say, which is why he was never hurting for a date back in high school. If anything, time has made him more handsome. Why does that happen with some men? The older they get, the sexier they become.

"This place is beautiful. You've really done well for yourself on a teacher's salary," I say as we walk toward the house.

He laughs under his breath. "I inherited it from my grandmother, actually. She passed away five years ago, and being the only grandchild has its perks, I suppose."

"You have a lot to be thankful for then."

"Yes, I most certainly do. Thankful is what I'm feeling today." I can tell he's looking at me, and I can see those pearly white teeth in my peripheral vision, but I stare forward like I'm marching in a very rigid parade.

I'm trying my best not to give him the wrong impression. We had some good times when we were teenagers, but we're all grown up now. And a relationship with Kent Akers isn't something on my mind no matter how good looking he is. Or how nice his house is. Or how much I'm craving a connection with a man who actually wants me too.

We walk inside, and it's more gorgeous than the outside. I see Tabitha chatting with a teacher I recognize from the school, and Harper is petting a very ugly Bulldog by the fireplace. As I imagined, there's a roaring blaze but the dog isn't the requisite Irish Setter I was envisioning. Instead, the pup has the worst underbite I've ever seen.

"Let me take your coat," Kent says as I slide it off my shoulders. "Make yourself at home. We have some appetizers in the kitchen and wine on the island." He pauses for a moment until I nod and make eye contact and then heads down a hallway to the right to put my coat away.

"Can you even believe this place?" Tabitha asks, suddenly appearing in front of me. I scan the room and take in the ornate features, yet it feels so homey. With thick wood moldings and original hardwood floors, I can feel the history of the home. But the kitchen has been updated and a wall has been opened between it and the living room, giving it a more modern feel.

"It's unreal. I had no idea this home was back here."

"Well of course not. We grew up on the other side of town," she says with a chuckle.

"You mean the poor side?"

"No. We weren't poor. We were just financially deficient."

I laugh at her sarcasm. "Look at Harper. She seems to love that dog."

"His name is Scooter," Kent says as he walks up behind me.

"Scooter? That's not a very masculine name," I remark with a smile.

"Agreed. My ex named him that."

"Ex? You were married?" I ask, surprised that anyone ever roped Kent Akers into marriage. I'd assumed he would always be a bachelor because his choices were too numerous to narrow down.

"Yep. For six years."

"What happened?" Tabitha pipes in, being her normal nosy self.

"Tabby!" I admonish her. It has never worked before, but I have hope that adulthood has made her more aware of people's feelings. She's never had a filter between her mouth and brain.

"It's okay. I don't mind the question. Her name was Michelle. We met at a baseball game. Had some good years. Had a couple of not so good years. Then she decided that she wanted to play for a different team altogether."

I bite my lip and wrinkle my nose. "Ouch."

"Yeah. Hard to compete with that."

I can see Tabitha struggling to hold in a laugh. "I'm going to go get some wine. Want anything?"

I shake my head and push her away, hoping Kent doesn't notice her face about the crack from the stifled laugh.

"Sorry. She can't help herself," I say. He seems unbothered.

"No problem. I've moved past it all, honestly. But it was a good humility check for me."

I smile. "I can imagine. I mean, I always think of you as this woman magnet…"

"So was my wife, unfortunately," he says, eliciting an immediate loud laugh on my part. I swear the whole room quiets for a moment, looks at me and then goes back to talking. My face feels like it's on fire. "Have I mentioned how glad I am that you're here, Indy?"

"Yeah… You might have mentioned it once or twice," I say, averting my eyes and looking around the room again.

"Look, I don't mean to make you feel uncomfortable. It's just that you're one of my biggest regrets in life, Indy Stone."

I freeze in place and turn to him, my eyebrows knitted together in confusion. "You regret taking me to prom?"

He laughs and touches my upper arm. "No! Of course not! I regret letting you get away from me."

Right now, I feel like running for one of the exits. Coming back to Peach Valley has been this strange mixed bag of an enjoyable walk down memory lane and a blast of frigid cold air hitting me right in the face.

He must sense my surprise at his words because he smiles and touches my arm again.

"Don't freak out. I just thought you should know I feel like an idiot for not realizing what a catch you were back then. I'm not asking for anything."

I smile gratefully. "Sorry. I was just shocked at what you said."

We both stand there nervously, fidgeting and looking around the room for a moment. I hate uncomfortable situations like this. Childhood was one long uncomfortable situation after another.

"Want some turkey?" he finally asks, almost too loudly. I nod and we head toward the kitchen, splitting up along the way. I glue myself to Tabitha's side without a word, and Harper eventually pulls herself away from Scooter long enough to join us for a quick prayer around the kitchen island.

Thankfully, the uncomfortable-ness of the day eventually dies down as I mingle and officially meet some of my co-workers. Single women and men mostly. People whose family were either too far away or estranged enough to not have a place to go for Thanksgiving. Not sure where I fit into that description.

Kent is keeping his distance for the most part, probably sensing my immediate reaction to his kind comment. I don't even know why it affected me that way. It was a nice thing to say that I was a "catch" back then, but I got the distinct feeling that there was more to it than that.

And I can't pretend that Dawson's face didn't flash in my mind. Our past. Our kiss. His inability or desire to have a future that includes official legal documents, a flower girl and tin cans bouncing on the ground behind our car as we head off into our life of bliss.

"That was fun," Tabitha says as we start putting the doggie bags Kent gave us in my refrigerator. There was enough turkey for a small army, and we got a lot of it to use as sandwiches for Harper's lunches.

"Yeah. It was."

"He's cute, you know," she says softly, not looking at me.

"Stop."

She pulls her head out of the refrigerator and looks at me. "Indy, you can't hold out hope for Dawson forever."

"Seriously? I'm not doing that, Tabby. I was married, for

goodness sakes. I hadn't thought of Dawson in years. One kiss certainly didn't make me fall head over heels in love with him. This isn't a romance novel."

"I don't buy it."

I shut the door to the refrigerator and look into the living room to make sure Harper hasn't come out of her bedroom. "Well, you don't have to buy it. Decades have passed, and I'm not looking for love with Dawson or anyone else. I have a new daughter to raise, and she is my only focus right now."

Tabitha shrugs her shoulders. "Fine. Whatever you say. But in the unlikely event that you do have some lingering feelings for Dawson, just know this," she says, putting her hands on my shoulders. "You deserve someone who loves you as much as you love them and sees no future without you in it."

"Noted," I say with a smile.

Tabitha leans against the counter, and I can tell she wants to say something else.

"I'm leaving."

"What? Already?"

She laughs. "I've already overstayed my welcome, Indy."

"You could never overstay your welcome. You know that," I say, holding both of her hands. "I've missed you so much all these years. I didn't even know how much."

"Ditto. But I'm like a feather floating on a breeze. Nothing can hold me down for long."

"You're quite the philosopher," I say with a giggle.

"One of my many talents. Look, the organizer of my Blue Ridge hike texted while we were at Kent's. The start date has been moved up, and I need to be at the planning meeting tomorrow. So, I've got to rent a car and get up there first thing in the morning."

"Let me at least drive you…"

"Nope. Better to say my goodbyes here."

"It's not goodbye."

She pulls me into a big hug and squeezes me tightly. "It's never goodbye for us."

We stand there in the kitchen, quietly hugging for several minutes before I feel the first tear stream down my cheek.

I SWING BACK AND FORTH, my feet lightly grazing the red clay below me. The memories of sitting on my wooden swing as a child are still fresh. Hours upon hours of laughter and singing with my boom box sitting in my lap. Those were innocent times.

Harper walks outside and sits down beside me. "Are you okay?" She has never asked me that before.

"Of course. Why do you ask?"

"Do you miss Tabitha?" She's only been gone a few hours, but Harper must sense my melancholy attitude.

I take in a breath. "I do. She's my best friend."

"Like me and Olivia."

"Yep. And best friends last forever no matter how many miles are between them."

"Olivia said that one day we'll be in each other's weddings. And she's going to have a little boy, and I'm going to have a little girl. And they're going to get married so we can be family forever."

I smile. "Sounds like a plan." We swing for a few moments without words until Harper breaks the silence.

"Sometimes, I miss my daddy."

If it's possible, I feel like someone is piercing my heart with an ice pick.

"I know you do, sweetie," I say, putting my arm around her. To my surprise, she puts her head on my shoulder.

"It was hard on Thanksgiving because I've never had one

without him there." My heart clenches in my chest, and I hold back the tears that are threatening to spill over.

"I'm so sorry, Harper. I didn't even think about that. I was so focused on making sure we all had a good day…"

"It's okay. I had fun. I really liked Scooter," she says with a giggle as she sits back up.

"Yeah, Scooter has one of those faces only a mother could love." He really is an incredibly ugly dog, which makes him even more lovable.

"Do you think my mother can see me from heaven?"

This kid is killing me today. Although I'm a counselor, I find it incredibly hard to get the distance I need to say the right things to her. Nothing feels right. I feel like I'm always tripping over my words.

"Of course I do, Harper. She's been watching over you your whole life."

"Do you think she and my Dad are together?" She's looking at me now, innocence showing in her eyes.

I take her hand in mine, and she lets me, which is nice. "I'd bet on it. They are watching you, and they're so proud of how you've handled yourself. I know I am."

"But I was a pain when I first came here," she says with a laugh.

"And that was understandable. All of this was new, and you didn't know me. I want to apologize to you, Harper."

"For what?"

"For not trying harder with your Daddy. I thought people couldn't really change, but I think your father did. Had I reached out, I would've known that. And I would have known you."

She bites her lip and then reaches out and hugs me tightly. "It's okay, Aunt Indy. We have the rest of our lives to get to know each other. Just don't leave me, okay?"

I can't form words, so I just hold her there and nod, my lips pressed to the top of her full head of red locks.

"Never," is all I can manage to choke out. And in that moment, I feel like I'm hugging my brother and apologizing for not fighting his demons with him.

"Can we get a puppy?"

"Oh, Harper... What am I going to do with you?" I say with a laugh.

CHAPTER 10

I'm tired of staring at this fig tree every day. But now that the leaves have fallen off, at least I can see through the branches. I decide that maybe it will be easier to trim the limbs now that the tree isn't covered in thick greenery.

"Don't you think you should hire somebody to do that?" Harper asks as she sits on the front porch sipping her hot chocolate. It's the Saturday after Thanksgiving, and while most women are shopping the sales at the mall, I'm wearing my rattiest jeans and an oversized sweatshirt, holding a giant saw in my hands.

"Nah. I did this all the time when I was a kid."

"Yeah, well, you're not a kid anymore," she says with a giggle.

"You better hush up, missy!" I say, throwing a stray, dead leaf in her direction. It leaves my hand and spirals to the ground, an anti-climactic ending to my toss.

"Harper! Do you want to go shopping with us?" Olivia yells from her rolled down car window. Her mother, Suzanne, smiles and waves at me. Harper gives me those pleading eyes and puts her hands together in a prayer position.

"Please?"

"But we were going to trim the fig tree," I say, trying to keep a straight face. Her smile falls. "Oh, good Lord, I was just kidding! You can go."

"Yes!" she says before running up to me, giving me a quick hug and then dashing off to Olivia's car. I wave goodbye again and then look back at the tree. Maybe Harper is right. Maybe I'm too old to be climbing trees alone while using large garden implements.

But that doesn't stop me. I decide which limb needs to be trimmed first, and of course it has to be the top one. Once I cut that one, I can work my way down.

I position my hiking boot on the bottom limb and start the ascent to the top of the behemoth of a tree. Taking my saw, I start with a couple of smaller limbs just to get a feel for the tool. It's harder to use than I expected, and the tiny little teeth are getting stuck in the hard wood.

"Dang it," I say out loud as I realize that the stupid saw is wedged between two pieces of wood. I pull hard and finally regain control of it before climbing higher. I dare not look down because I'm definitely not a huge fan of heights, but the job has to be done. A single woman has to know how to do these things. Change a tire, check her oil, kill a bear.

I finally reach the highest limb, the one I came for. The ultimate trophy. Maybe I'll cut it and have it mounted so I can hang it on my bedroom wall. I press the saw into the limb and immediately realize that this flimsy little thing probably isn't going to do the job. Maybe Harper was right and I should have hired someone, but it's too late now. I've managed to get the saw about a quarter of the way into the wood, but it isn't going any further no matter what I do.

And then one of those moments happens where you don't

really know what happened. I pull on the saw in an effort to get it out of the wood so I can climb back down and look up tree trimmers on my wonderful phone. Instead, when I pull on it, I lose my grip, tumbling down through the tree limbs like a pinball hitting every obstacle along the way.

When I land, it's in the middle of the tree where all of the limbs converge together at the base. I'm in pain in so many areas that I can't think straight.

"Help! Help!" I call out, worried that I might pass out from the pain at any moment. I have no other way to get help since my phone is on the porch. "Help!"

"Indy! Oh my God! What happened?" I hear Dawson saying as he starts to push the limbs away like they're toothpicks in an effort to get to me. It dawns on me that he got there awfully fast.

"I fell from the top..." I manage to mumble. My eyes are getting heavy, and I'm talking softer than I mean to.

"Does anything hurt?" he asks as he crouches in the tree with me.

"Everything hurts..."

I can feel him touching different parts of me. I wonder if I'm bleeding, but I can't get the energy to even ask. Why am I so tired?

"Stay awake, Indy. I'm going to get you help okay? You're going to be okay." He sounds so sure, yet terrified. I can hear his voice shaking as he makes a call. And then my mind goes blank.

The next memory I have includes lots of beeping noises and bright lights. When I finally manage to open my eyes fully, I recognize the emergency department at Peach Valley Hospital. I have a faint memory of getting stitches here once when I was a kid, and not much has changed.

"Oh, thank God. You're awake. You scared me to death," Dawson says. He's sitting beside the bed, one of his hands holding mine and the other rubbing my forehead. I've never heard his voice sound so strained, so full of emotion. And the look on his face is one of sheer relief.

"I'm so sore," I say. It feels like someone kicked me in the head, and then for good measure they hit me with a baseball bat on my arms and legs. Even my ribs hurt.

"You took quite a tumble, Miss Stone," the doctor says above me. "Thankfully, it's mostly bruising, but you do have a slight concussion. So we're going to keep you overnight for observation, and then you need to stay off your feet for at least a week."

"Harper?" I say to Dawson.

"She's fine. Staying with Olivia. I just texted her and told her you're awake."

I turn my attention back to the doctor. "I can't take a week off work…"

He gives me a stern look. "You can and you will. You were very lucky that this young man found you so quickly. It could've been a really serious situation."

After he walks out of the room, I look at Dawson. "My hero."

He smiles. "Don't you know by now that I will always do what I can to help you, Indy? No matter what."

"How did you get there so fast? Were you watching me be an idiot?" My throat feels like I've been gargling rocks, and those little things shooting oxygen up my nose are highly uncomfortable.

"Nope. I happened to walk outside to check the mail when I saw you climbing up the tree. I was worried about you, so I started walking up to your house to tell you it wasn't a good idea… Then you started yelling for help…" His voice is shakier than I expected. "You scared me, Indy. I never want to hear you yelling for help like that again, okay?"

"I'll try," I say with a soft laugh. He leans in and looks at me, not an ounce of amusement on his face.

"I'm serious. You need help, you call me. You don't do things that could get you hurt. I can't deal with it. Okay?"

"Okay, Dawson. I'm sorry. It's going to be alright." I don't know why he's so upset, but then I've been out like a light for awhile now. In fact, I have no idea what time it is. "How long was I asleep?"

"About three hours."

"Three hours? Wow."

"Longest three hours of my life..." I hear him say under his breath before he lays his head down on my upper arm. A few moments later, I can hear him lightly snoring.

~

"CAN I get you anything else? More water?" he asks as he stands in my bedroom doorway. After leaving the hospital, the doctor gave me strict instructions to stay in bed for one week, and Dawson intends to stand guard to make sure that happens.

"I'm fine, Dawson. I promise. See? I've got the two bottles of water you gave me as back up." I hold up the two plastic bottles and shake them a bit, smiling at his doting nature. "Don't you need to get to work?"

He shakes his head. "No. I took the week off. I'm not leaving your side, Indy Stone." He sits at the end of my bed.

"Dawson, you can't take a week off. I'm okay. If I need something major, I can call Lisa. She's just across the street and she offered..."

"I'm staying here. Besides, I've never taken a vacation day at the school, so they owe me a lot of days."

"This isn't a vacation."

"Anywhere with you is a vacation for me," he says before

standing up and adjusting the mini blinds to bring in more light. "Any idea what you want for lunch?"

"Filet mignon?" I tease.

He raises an eyebrow. "Say the word."

"I think a grilled cheese sandwich and sweet tea would be sufficient." I'm truly afraid he'll actually go get filet mignon for lunch.

I still feel really sore, so the doctor prescribed some pain pills for me. With my family history, I refuse to take them but I know they're available if the pain gets worse. For now, I'll just use ibuprofen.

"Want to watch TV? I also brought some DVDs in case you haven't seen these movies…"

"You're a really good nurse, Dawson Woods." He turns and smiles at me.

"I just want to make sure that you're okay."

"I am. But I hate that you're wasting your vacation on me."

He walks toward me and sits down beside me. "I wondered about you for years, Indy. I thought I might never see you again. There is truly no place I'd rather be than right here, sitting on the edge of your bed." I can hear the emotion in his voice.

"Dawson, what's wrong? You seem way more upset about this accident than I am."

He takes in a deep breath. "When I heard you screaming for help, it did things to me. I couldn't get my feet to move fast enough. I felt so unequipped to help you…"

"But you did help me."

"Indy, there were things happening in that moment that happen to me a lot."

"What do you mean?"

"I could hear sounds from when I was in Iraq. Everything around me changed from this serene little neighborhood to

133

the desert. I could see bombs going off in the distance. I could feel the ground shaking under my feet…"

"You have PTSD." I don't ask it as a question. I declare it as a fact. I'm a therapist, and I know PTSD when I hear it.

He nods his head silently. "So when I heard you screaming for help, I went into survival mode. Serena screamed just before…" He's staring straight ahead again, stuck in some place that I can't see or access.

"Dawson…"

"I felt so guilty that you fell out of that tree."

"Guilty? I'm the moron who chose to climb up there."

He finally looks at me. "I should've seen you sooner and stopped you. Or I shouldn't have walked out that morning just because you said what you did."

I lean up enough to touch his arm. "I shouldn't have abandoned you on Thanksgiving. I felt so bad that you were alone, but I couldn't come over there and face you."

"I wasn't alone."

My stomach clenches up at the thought of him spending the day with a woman, a sensation I wasn't expecting. I sent him away, after all. How can I be jealous?

"Oh?"

"I volunteered at the soup kitchen," he says. My body relaxes again. That's just like Dawson - giving to others even when he's hurting himself. "And you?"

I clear my throat and look down at my hands. "We went to Kent's house." I see him slowly nod his head and turn slightly. "He has this thing every year where he invites people that have nowhere else to go… Other teachers mainly…"

"Well, that was very nice of Kent. I'm sure you had a good time." He stands up and adjusts the blinds again, although they don't need to be adjusted. I can feel the tension in the room.

"It wasn't like that, Dawson."

He turns and runs his fingers through his hair. I can see his jaw clenching from across the room. "Wasn't like what?"

"There's nothing going on between me and Kent. He's an old friend. That's all."

"Look, Indy, your love life isn't any of my business." I don't know why that statement feels like a stab in my heart, but it does.

"You know what? You're absolutely right about that." I turn onto my side and close my eyes. "I need some rest. Can you just give me some time to myself?"

He doesn't say a word, but I hear the door close quietly a few moments later. I've never had such a whirlwind of feelings inside, and right now none of them feel good.

MY STOMACH IS GROWLING which indicates that it must be getting close to dinnertime. I didn't mean to sleep this long, but rest is the only thing I've been instructed to do by the doctor. I can see shards of pink and orange light peeking through the mini blinds that Dawson kept rearranging before I fell asleep.

Dawson.

I feel horrible about the way we left things. I bet he went home and decided to just leave me alone.

"Good evening, sleepyhead," I hear him say from across the room. He's sitting on the floor, his back against the closet doors, watching me.

"How long have you been sitting there?"

He ambles up to his feet, grunting like an old man as he stretches his lower back. "Long enough to realize I'm getting too old to sit on the floor."

I smile sleepily and rub my eyes. "Where's Harper?"

"Doing her homework and eating a grilled cheese sandwich."

"You're a regular Mr. Mom," I say, easing myself up to a seated position. "I'm sorry I cut you off earlier."

He walks over and sits next to me on the bed. "No, that was totally my fault, Indy. I just… Well, knowing you spent Thanksgiving with Kent made me… jealous." I can tell saying the words are hard for him.

"Jealous? But why?"

"Don't you get it?"

"Apparently not," I say, getting frustrated. I feel like he's talking in riddles.

He takes my hands in his. "I've loved you since the day I met you, Indy Stone."

I can't breathe. Maybe I have a blood clot in my lungs that they didn't catch because I truly can't breathe in or out. I'm frozen. Just great. I'm paralyzed. The sexiest man in America just told me he loves me, and I look like one of those wax figures at the museum that creep me out so much.

"Indy? You okay?"

"Yeah," I manage to eek out, my breath finally returning to me. "Love?" Now I can only speak in one word sentences. That should make the rest of my life interesting.

He smiles, and I suddenly notice the stubble that has formed around his chiseled jawline. Dang, that's nice.

"Yes, love. When I saw you in my classroom… God, I thought I was hallucinating. I could barely breathe. I tried to be cool, but there you were. Indy Stone. In the flesh. And every single emotion and feeling that I'd tried to push away since I was twelve years old came rushing back. It was like my life was this big puzzle with one missing piece, and there it was."

"Me?"

"Yes, you," he says with a laugh. He looks down and rubs

his thumb across the top of my hand. It feels nice. "And when I saw you talking to Kent that day... Well, some other feelings came back. Fierce protection. The desire to punch his lights out..."

"We were only talking, Dawson."

"I know. And I get that I have no right to tell you who to love."

"What? I don't love Kent. I never did. He was just my prom date," I say with a laugh. "He wore a tuxedo with a glittery teal bow tie. He got drunk at the after prom party and threw up on my shoe. I can assure you I do not love Kent."

He smiles, but only slightly. "I know you don't love Kent Akers. But he definitely likes you as more than a friend, and hearing that you spent Thanksgiving over there... Well, it just felt like a knife in my heart." He stands up and paces across the room, running his fingers through his hair again. "But see, I also know that I can't offer you what you want, so I'm having a hard time reconciling my feelings here, Indy."

"What do you think I want?"

"Marriage and all the stuff that comes with it."

"We literally just saw each other again. I'm not ready for marriage. To anyone."

"No, but you said it yourself the other day. You don't want to start something with me when we both know it won't end the way you want." He stands up and walks to the window, staring out at the nothingness.

My stomach is churning again. I hate when he says stuff like that. And I hate that it bothers me so much. I'm a grown woman. I'm a professional therapist. I don't *need* a man to be whole. But I sure do *want* this one. I always have.

"You're right. I did say that. And I did mean it."

He looks at me as if he's expecting me to say more, but I literally bite my tongue inside my mouth to keep from going back on what I said. After all, how bad would it be to date without worrying about marriage? Maybe I could change his mind at some point?

Jeez, I need a therapist myself.

"I'm going to put on my therapist's hat for a moment."

"Oh great."

I pat the edge of my bed, and he sits back down. "You don't love me, Dawson. The twelve year old little boy who needed a friend loves me, but you don't. You're a grown man who has been to war and is now rebuilding his life. I've been a blast from your past, and it has stirred up intense emotions, but that doesn't mean it's love."

"I do love you. I know what it feels like, Indy."

"Just hear me out," I say, wanting to kiss him hard but pushing my own feelings away. "I think you're afraid of losing this - our bond - all over again, so you react a little badly when you think someone might take me away from you. But I'm here, Dawson. I'm not going anywhere. And we're adults now, so you never have to lose touch with me again. We're friends..."

Before I can finish saying anything, he leans in and kisses me hard on the lips, preventing me from talking. It's not a sexual kiss, but one to basically shut me up. When he pulls back, he puts his index finger over my lips.

"No. I love you. Period. End of story. And it's okay that you don't feel that way about me, Indy, because if somebody has to get hurt, I'd rather it be me. And I'd rather have you in my life and always ache for you to love me back than to not have you at all."

I want to tell him I love him, but what good would that do? Because he's right - we want different outcomes, and I've experienced enough heartbreak in my life. So friendship has to be the only bond we have, even though it's quite apparent that we both feel more.

"Dawson, I..."

"How are you feeling?" Harper says from the bedroom door. I smile at the sight of her. It's hard to believe, but when I see her I don't think of her as my niece. I truly think of her as my daughter.

"Hey, sweetie. I'm feeling better this evening, actually," I say. It's a lie. My body feels a thousand pounds heavier than normal, and I've got a splitting headache over my right eye for some reason.

"I made chocolate chip cookies if you want some," she says, holding up a plate piled high with cookies.

"Yum," Dawson says as he reaches over to take one.

"Ladies first, Mr. Woods!" Harper corrects, pulling the plate back. Dawson laughs.

"You've been well taught, young lady. I was going to give this one to your…"

"Mom?" Harper asks. The room falls silent for a moment.

"Aunt Indy," I say, not wanting her to feel pressured.

"I like Mom better," she says softly before turning and walking back down the hallway. My eyes bug out of my head, and I can't help but grin from ear to ear.

"Mom," I say to myself, and Dawson just smiles at me.

WHEN I OPEN my eyes again, I can see it's almost eleven at night. The TV is still flickering with a rerun of Friends, and Dawson is on the floor with his head hanging to the side, eyes closed.

"Dawson," I whisper loudly. He doesn't budge. I toss an extra throw pillow at him, nailing him directly on the top of his head and scaring the bejesus out of him. He looks around in confusion for a moment before realizing where he is.

"You okay?" he asks, rubbing his eyes. "Need more water?" Why does he always assume I'm dehydrated?

"No. I need you to go home and get some sleep. You've been here since early this morning."

"I'm not going home. I'm not leaving you until you're all healed up," he says as he starts to close his eyes again.

"Dawson, you need rest, and my floor isn't restful. You're going to have an awful crick in your neck."

"Well, I won't rest if I don't know you're okay anyway."

I consider the living room sofa, but it's so modern with its hard edges that there's no way Dawson would even be able to lie down on it. I look around my bedroom. There's really nowhere for him to relax. My room is small, a side effect of a 70's ranch house. I don't even have a reading chair in here. But I do have a queen sized bed.

For a moment, I consider Harper and what she might think if she sees her teacher snuggled in my bed. But I know she's asleep, and a freight train won't wake that kid up. Tomorrow she catches the bus at eight AM, and she's careful not to wake me up, opting to get herself ready and fed before running to the bus that stops right in front of our house.

I can't let him sleep like this - on the floor in a heap like a homeless person outside the airport. All he needs is a pile of newspapers to use as a blanket and he'd fit the part quite nicely.

Yet there's a part of me that knows it would be dangerous for both of us to be that close.

"Dawson?"

"Yeah?" he says, startled again.

"Come up here and get in bed with me."

His eyes pop open. "Excuse me?"

"If you insist on staying here, then you need actual rest. So either go home or get in this bed."

"I... um..."

"Relax. We're friends, remember? And I'm in far too much

pain to be the sex goddess you're dreaming of right now anyway."

He smiles. "Fine. But try to keep your hands off me."

He stands and locks the door, probably thinking about Harper. Then he does something I don't expect. He strips off his t-shirt and walks to the bed, his chiseled muscles on full display. When did he start looking like *that*? All I remember is the gangly boy I once knew. He has definitely filled out since then.

Thankfully, he keeps his jeans on because I don't know if I could resist him in boxers or briefs.

This is going to be the longest night of my life.

CHAPTER 11

The room is dark, minus the sliver of moonlight peeking through the mini blinds. I can hear Dawson breathing lightly next to me as I check the clock. It's 3AM.

I'm normally a great sleeper, but I'm no longer used to sleeping next to a man. Especially not a man that I find almost impossible to resist. And there he is with his well-defined chest muscles and actual six pack.

David never had a six pack. He's tall and thin and wiry, and his stomach caves in. He's more of an academic type, so I can't imagine a time when he would've focused on being in shape. The thought of him makes me want to throw up, so I push his image from my mind.

It's so hard to get comfortable with my injuries, and I can tell the ibuprofen wore off long ago. I can't take anymore tonight, so I have to find a way to get settled. I slowly turn to my left to face the door of my room, adjusting my pillow as I turn.

But when I do, Dawson rouses and turns with me, mumbling something in his sleep. I freeze in place, not wanting to wake him up, but I have to finish my turn because right now it hurts. So I roll as quickly as I can and before I know it, he's wrapped around me.

His arm is around my body. His lips are pressed to the back of my head. His leg is slung over mine. I'm wrapped in a cocoon of Dawson. And I've never felt so incredibly peaceful as I do right now, like no one and nothing can ever touch me. Protected. Loved.

Ugh. I've got to stop this.

I can feel his warm breath on the back of my head. He pulls me tighter, a moan escaping from his lips. I feel like his own personal stuffed teddy bear as he grips me into a strong embrace.

But now I'm finding it a little difficult to breathe. I don't want him to move. I love this feeling. It gives me a moment to pretend we're a couple. A normal couple in love, and not one that can't be together. It lets me live inside of my own fantasy, romance novel world. Doing this while he's awake would be a recipe for disaster, but he doesn't know what he's doing right now and I want to enjoy the sensations.

Only I really can't breathe well.

"Dawson?" I whisper as I slightly turn my head. He immediately wakes up and lifts his head.

"Everything okay?" he says, his voice gruff and gravely.

"Yeah. Well, no, actually. You're holding me a little tight..."

I can see out of my peripheral vision that he suddenly realizes what he's done, and he lets go. He moves back a good foot.

"I'm so sorry, Indy. Did I hurt you?"

"No. Not at all. I was just having a little trouble breathing," I say as I turn to face him. He looks horrified.

"Are you sure you're okay?"

I reach out and touch his arm. "Dawson, I'm totally fine. I was actually…"

"What?"

"Enjoying it. I enjoyed having you wrapped around me like that." I should not have said that. I immediately regret sending him a mixed signal.

"Oh yeah?" he says in a low voice, taunting me. "You kind of liked being my personal teddy bear?"

What is he, reading my mind?

"Good night, Dawson," I say, turning back toward the door.

I can feel him sliding closer until my back is pressed against his front. I'm trying to ignore certain "reactions" his body is having to mine, but it's not working. He doesn't put his leg over me, but he does slide his arm back around me and then lays his cheek against the top of my head.

I turn my head just enough to look into his eyes. We freeze there for a moment. He leans down and kisses me slowly on my forehead. Then he moves to one cheek and then the other. He looks at me for a moment, lingering awfully close to my lips. And then he lightly kisses the tip of my nose instead.

"Good night, Indy," he whispers before he kisses the top of my head and then lays his head back down.

I'm not sure I'll ever sleep again.

When I wake up the next morning, Harper has already gone to school and Dawson is missing from my bed. Not a good start to the day.

The doctor was right about me being more sore as the days go on. There is no way I could've worked this week with the level of pain I have. Who knew falling out of a tree could be so painful?

I struggle to sit myself up in bed just as I hear a knock at the bedroom door. Dawson never knocks; I think he's hoping I'll be changing my shirt or something, so he always comes barging in with a big grin on his face.

"Come in," I say, assuming it's Lisa coming for a visit.

Instead, I see a face I haven't seen in years and one I didn't expect to see at all. Amy.

"Amy? Oh my gosh, what are you doing here?" I ask, genuinely shocked that I'm happy to see her. I convince myself that it's always nice to see a familiar face.

She looks overwrought with concern, her eyebrows squished together with worry. It's weird because she was never concerned about me when we were kids.

"Oh, Indy! Are you okay?" she asks, running to my bedside like I'm dying of some terrible disease and have just minutes to live.

"I'm fine, Amy. You didn't have to come all the way across the country…"

"When I saw Lisa asking for prayers on Facebook, I couldn't believe it was about you…" She puts her hand to her chest and sits down and then starts rubbing her hand across my forehead. It feels motherly, and I haven't known this side of her. At first, I wonder if it's an act, but then I remember what a horrible actress Amy was. She literally got kicked out of a high school play for being what her theater teacher called "unable to properly relay human emotions".

"Lisa asked for prayers on Facebook?" I had no idea my falling out of the fig tree was such big news. Welcome to Peach Valley.

"What did the doctor say? What can I do?"

She seriously seems distraught, and I feel worse for her than I do for myself.

"Amy, listen," I say, holding up my hands. "I'm okay. You're really overreacting for nothing."

Behind her, in the doorway, I see Dawson standing there with a smile on his face.

"I see you've met my sister?" I say to him. Amy turns and looks at him and then back at me.

"Is that your boyfriend?" she whispers rather loudly.

"No. He's just an old friend," I whisper back even louder. Dawson chuckles and walks back up the hallway. "Amy, what are you doing here?"

She smiles and sighs. "I've been a horrible sister to you, Indy. I guess when I heard you'd been hurt, I just freaked. We've already lost our brother and our parents... Well, we're all that's left."

Her eyes are filling with tears which shocks me to my core. The only time I ever saw Amy cry was when her boyfriends would break up with her, and even then she would get herself together and plot her revenge against them later the same day.

"I haven't exactly tried to be the best sister to you either," I say, trying to extend my own olive branch. And it's true. Just because she's older doesn't mean I'm blameless in all of this.

"I know I treated you like a lowly little sister when we were kids, Indy. I was such a brat," she says with a laugh through her tears.

"I can't really argue with that one." That elicits an even bigger laugh from her.

"I was so happy to hear from you when you called, even though it wasn't with happy news about Danny. But I have three kids, and being a mother has taught me a lot."

"Oh yeah? Like what?"

"You know, I've seen my kids argue many times. But as a mother, it absolutely breaks my heart when I hear them say ugly things to each other. I realized that the same thing that breaks my heart now must've broken your heart as a kid. I don't even let my kids call each other 'stupid' or 'brat', yet I called you those things regularly. I've wanted to apologize for so long, Indy, but I didn't think you'd want to talk to me."

I can feel the pain in her words, and I don't think I've ever been so shocked in my life. Amy really feels bad, and she wants to make amends. A part of me wonders if Danny is somewhere orchestrating this - the reconnecting of his family.

"I hope you'll accept my apology," she says softly, reaching for both of my hands. "I'm not who I used to be, and I'd like the chance to be your sister."

Now my own eyes are watering. "Of course I accept your apology, Amy. I won't lie. You did hurt me as a kid, but we're grown women now, and we can make different choices."

She reaches out and hugs me tightly. I don't have the heart to tell her that my medicine has worn off and my shoulder is killing me. Thankfully, she lets me go moments later.

"Now, where's that niece of mine?" she asks with a smile as she wipes her eyes.

"Still at school. She usually gets home around three-thirty."

Amy looks at her watch. "Oh. It's not even ten yet. Well, what can I do to help you?"

I pause for a moment to think and then smile. "Do you like eighties movies?"

"Of course. Why?"

"How about we do a sister thing right now and you climb up here and watch a movie marathon with me?"

Her eyes get wide. "Really?"

"That would be the best medicine for me right now."

Without question, Amy crawls up into the bed, snuggles

up next to me and we start with Pretty in Pink. Having a sister might not be so bad after all.

∽

AFTER WATCHING TWO MOVIES, I send Amy out to get lunch for us and for Dawson who has been hovering around the house all day. I've heard the vacuum running a couple of times, and I think I spotted him wearing my apron in the hallway once.

"You know, Peach Valley is a very healing place," I say as he dusts my dresser for the umpteenth time.

"What do you mean?"

"Well, since I've been back, I've met my niece and forged a relationship with her. I've seen Tabitha. I've reunited with you. I've made peace with this house. Amy came back..."

"A lot has changed in Peach Valley..." he says in a dramatic tone as if he's doing the voice-over for a soap opera.

"You know what I mean. I hated the thought of moving back here. It felt like failure. Or reliving the past. But it has brought so much healing to my heart, Dawson."

He smiles and sits down beside me. "Does that mean you'll stay here for good? Give up Charleston and that salty ocean breeze?"

"I don't know if I can promise that just yet, but I have decided to unpack my last suitcase if that makes you feel any better."

"Food has arrived!" I hear Amy yelling from the kitchen. What a flashback to our childhood when I would hear her yelling all sorts of things around the house.

I start to stand up, but Dawson steps in front of me. "No. Sit down. I'll bring it."

"Dawson, I have to start moving. I'm getting stiff being in this bed so much."

"Tomorrow. Just give it one more day, okay?"

I sigh and sit back down. "Fine. But tomorrow I'm getting up."

"Yes, ma'am," he says as he salutes me. A few minutes later, he returns with a sub sandwich, a bag of chips and sweet tea.

"I'm getting so bored," I say as he and Amy plop down on the floor beside my bed. "You know, you two are welcome to eat at the kitchen table like human beings."

Amy laughs. "I flew all the way to Peach Valley to check on my little sister, so I'll stay right here."

"And I walked two houses up here, so I'll stay too."

"You live two houses away?" Amy asks with a sly grin.

"Don't start. You're barking up the wrong tree," I warn as I take a bite of my sandwich.

"Let's not talk about trees," Dawson interjects. We all have a good laugh at that as we enjoy our meals and reminisce about old times. Each of our stories are very different, but we all share the bond of Peach Valley.

I HEAR the bus come down the street. Amy looks nervous as she sits on the edge of my bed.

"What if she hates me?"

"She might."

"Thanks a lot!" she says, lightly slapping my calf.

"We had a rough time at first, but we have a much better relationship now. It might take her awhile to warm up. She may have… questions."

"I'd like to spend some time with her. Get to know her. If you don't mind?"

"I think that would be great. We just need to go at her speed."

Amy nods, and I hear the front door open. Dawson has gone to run some errands.

"I'm home," she calls out.

"Hey, Harper, can you come here a minute?" I call back.

She appears in my doorway and glances at Amy before looking back at me. "Yes, ma'am?"

"Harper, this is my sister, Amy. Your other aunt," I say with a smile. My stomach knots up as I wait to hear her response. She surprises me by smiling ever so slightly.

"Hi. Nice to meet you. You look more like my Dad than Aunt Indy."

Amy sighs with relief and stands to hug Harper. I hold my breath hoping that she allows such a forward show of affection from someone she's just met. She quickly glances at me, as if seeking approval, and I nod.

Amy kisses the top of her head and releases her grip. "You know, you have some cousins who really want to meet you."

"I do?"

"Yes. I have two daughters and a son."

"Are they my age?"

"Well, Abigail is ten. Cammie is eight and Stuart is five."

"Are they here too?"

"No, sweetie. They're back in Seattle, but we're going to be seeing a lot more of each other now." Amy looks at me and I nod in agreement that we will be making more of an effort now that some scars have been healed.

"I can't believe I have cousins," Harper says with a grin. "That's like *real* family."

It hits me how much Harper has missed having a family. We all have. Some reasons for the estrangement had been valid. Others had been plain stupid. I guess that's how many families end up. Stupid fights. Stupid judgements. Stupid grudges being held from years gone by.

But there's pure love in this room right now, and the feeling almost overwhelms me. We could've had this years ago had someone stepped up and been the hero.

~

THE NEXT TWO days pass quickly with Dawson coming in and out checking on me while my sister takes the lead. I feel him stepping back, allowing us time to get to know each other again.

Part of me is glad that he's not with me 24/7 because it's too hard to ignore my feelings for him when he's around. The other part of me hates sleeping with Amy because she's a cover hog and doesn't give me the same secure feeling that Dawson does. Plus, she snores like a freight train.

Thankfully, I'm no longer relegated to my bed all day. I've been getting up and spending hours on the living room sofa. I even made myself some soup one day, but Dawson caught me and sent me back to the sofa. I think he enjoys taking care of me.

"When are you going back to work?" I ask him as he finally sits down beside me on the sofa. Amy has gone out to do some grocery shopping for me.

"Never. What if I just become your full-time house boy?" he says with that boyish grin that makes me want to do things I cannot do.

"Don't make promises you can't keep," I say, trying to keep my response light. His smile fades a bit and he leans his head against my shoulder.

"I would never want you to get hurt like this again, but I have to say I've enjoyed taking care of you, Indy."

"Oh yeah? Shall I climb the fig tree again next week?"

He looks at me. "Seriously, if you ever climb even one branch into that tree again, I'll take you over my knee."

"Again with the promises…" I know I shouldn't have said that, but it was too good to pass up.

He licks his lips and sighs before laying his head back against the sofa this time. "Do you think this will ever get any easier?"

"What?"

"Being around each other?"

"It's not easy to be around me?"

He sits up and puts his head in his hands. "Not for me." I watch him stand up and pace the room for a moment, obviously trying to gather his thoughts. "Sometimes, you make me believe it's possible."

"What's possible?"

"The whole thing. Love. Marriage. Kids. The white picket fence."

I feel my face flushing, but I don't want to move. I need him to keep talking.

"But then I remember my mother."

The wind blows right out of my sails. "You're not your mother, Dawson."

He sits down in a chair across the room. "I know that logically, Indy. But I saw - and experienced - a lot as a kid."

"I know…"

"No. You don't." He says it sharply. "You only know very little."

I grieve for him in this moment. I know what it's like to have secrets. What it's like to have pain that you can't name or talk about. And I wonder how we lived just two doors down from each other for months, and I still don't know what he was experiencing in that house.

"Dawson, have you ever considered counseling?" I ask softly.

"What?"

"I think it might help…"

He laughs in exasperation. "So now you think I'm crazy because I don't want to fall into the marriage trap?"

My mouth drops open. I can tell by the look on his face that he's immediately sorry he said that, but I don't give him a chance to speak. Instead, I pull myself up to my feet and hold my hands up to keep him from trying to help me.

"Now, you listen here, Dawson Woods! Don't put words in my mouth. I'm not trying to convince you to get married. But as your *friend*, I know you need help with your PTSD. Not just from war, but from the life you lived as a child. There are parts of you that are broken, and there's help for you."

He stands to face me. "I'm so sorry I said…"

"Seeking counseling doesn't make you crazy. What makes you crazy is reliving a past that's no longer happening and using other people's mistakes to justify your own… and then refusing to get help to make your present life better!"

"Indy, I…"

"Enough. I don't want to talk about this anymore. But just know this, Dawson. I'm not some desperate female looking to get married. Been there. Done that. Got the divorce decree to prove it. But I didn't get divorced because marriage is bad. I got divorced because I married the wrong man."

With that, I walk to my room and shut the door behind me before breaking down.

CHAPTER 12

*G*etting back to work has been both good and hard. It has been nice to see all of the kids again and get back to a sense of normalcy. I had no idea how much I missed their faces.

But it has also been difficult in that I'm still sore. Sitting behind my desk ends up making me feel stiff most days, so I'm looking forward to the winter break that is quickly approaching in a few days. I need some time off to enjoy family life without being laid up in my bed the whole time.

Once Amy knew I was okay, she headed back to Seattle. We're planning to get the kids together a few weeks after the Christmas holiday, and I know Harper is really looking forward to that.

"Well, I'm so glad to see you sitting back behind that desk again," Kent says after appearing in the doorway to my office. I've been avoiding him since Thanksgiving because I don't want to send him any mixed signals, but I think my very presence in the school is doing that for some reason. I definitely don't remember him being so focused on me back in high school.

"Glad to be back. Oh, and thanks for the flowers. They were lovely." He sent me a dozen roses almost before I made it home from the hospital. Dawson put them on the back patio for some reason. They never had a chance.

"I was going to come by... But I heard Dawson was taking care of you?"

"Yes. He was a godsend," I say with a quick smile. "So, what's up?"

He pushes away from the doorframe and walks to sit down in the chair across from my desk. Seeing that he plans to stay for a bit, I put down my pen and take a sip of my morning coffee.

"I don't know if you've heard, but there's a group of us going camping this weekend up in the mountains. Harper asked me why she wasn't invited when she saw me in the hallway just now."

"She did?"

"Apparently, some of the kids in her class were talking about it. I hadn't mentioned it to you because of your accident, but I wanted you to know that you two are more than welcome to join us..."

I chuckle. "I'm not much of a camper."

"Neither am I, honestly. But Brett Hawkins set this whole thing up, and if I don't go then he'll never let me live it down."

Brett is well known around school for being the "sportiest" teacher. He rock climbs, runs marathons and is training to compete in the Iron Man competition. He's not "big as a minute", as my mother would say, but he can move like lightning.

"We've got about ten kids going, along with their parents, of course. Several teachers. Lots of tents. Big campfire. Beautiful creek next to the campsite. I think Harper would really enjoy it. Her friend, Olivia, is going too."

I bite my lip. I want Harper to have these experiences. I know Danny would want me to let her go, but I'm not letting her go alone. How I wish Tabitha was still around because she's the perfect person for this adventure. She lives for bugs and dirt and the sound of coyotes howling in the distance. I live for nice hotels, soft sheets and plush bath towels.

I guess this is what single motherhood will be like. Giving up what I want so that Harper can have what she needs.

"Okay. Sure."

"Really?" he says, a look of shock on his face. "I was ready to keep pleading my case."

I smile. "Well, feel free to bribe me with a high-priced coffee drink or some chocolates."

Kent laughs. "Done." I was just joking. He stands up and walks toward the door. "Shall I tell Harper the good news?" he asks when he reaches the doorway.

"Go right ahead."

Before he leaves, he turns back. "Oh, and Indy? I can't wait for this weekend. It's going to be a blast."

I don't respond, opting instead to smile and take another sip of my coffee. But when I look back up, Kent is no longer standing there. Dawson is. And it's apparent that he just heard what Kent said.

"Good morning," he says, his face impassable.

"Good morning." I look back down at my papers, but he doesn't move.

"Listen, I just thought you should know that I'll be out of town for a few days. I'm leaving Friday."

I want to ask where he's going. But I'm still mad and hurt, so I don't.

"Okay. Safe travels."

He hovers for a moment before turning back toward the hallway. But then he turns back.

"And you have a very fun weekend, Indy."

Before I can look up, he's gone.

~

"HOW MUCH FURTHER IS IT?" Harper asks for the tenth time since we left home. It's only an hour drive, but it sure seems longer when she keeps asking questions.

"Should be right up here on the left," I say, glancing down at my navigation system while we wait at a red light.

I finally spot the campground and turn in. It's definitely not glamorous, but I didn't expect it to be. There are lots of cars in the lot, along with some campers and nicer motorhomes.

We park near the office, which is just a small cabin in the corner of the parking lot. As soon as I open my door, Kent is standing there like Johnny on the spot, ready to help me unload our bags. I packed light, as instructed.

"Welcome to paradise!" Kent says with a sarcastic laugh as he takes my duffel bag.

"How bad is it?"

"Actually, not too bad. Our campsite is a bit of a walk, so I hung out up here just to make sure you didn't get lost."

"Thanks," I say, trying not to make eye contact.

"Everyone is here. A few of the guys are already building the campfire. I'll help you and Harper set up your tent."

"My tent?" I say with my eyes wide.

"Yeah. You did bring a tent, right?"

I stop dead in my tracks. "No."

Kent laughs. "Indy, we're camping. Didn't you think you'd need a tent?"

I cover my eyes with my hand. "I thought tents were already here. I told you, I'm not a camper." I'm panicking now.

He puts his hand on my shoulder. "Look, we'll work it

out. I'm sure we can find accommodations for both of you." He smiles that toothy grin and winks before leading us down the long hiking trail to our campsite.

THE AREA where we're camping is nicer than I anticipated, with a beautiful creek and lush greenery surrounding the campsite. It's like a little oasis in the middle of the forest.

But it's still very rustic. It's not the Four Seasons, by any stretch. Because we're so far into the woods, there is no bathroom. I don't know why I didn't anticipate this. Thankfully, because we're such a large group, there is an outhouse available to us. Can't wait to try that out. Not.

Harper is enjoying herself already. I love to see her running around, laughing with her friends. Making new ones. It makes my heart smile. I never understood what that phrase meant until just now.

"Hot chocolate?" Kent asks as he sits down next to me on a log by the campfire. It's cool outside, so I pull my cardigan tighter around me. I might need to go retrieve my fleece jacket soon.

"Thanks," I say, reaching up and taking the Styrofoam cup from his hands. Harper runs over and roasts a marshmallow before heading back to the creek where the other kids are. It's almost pitch black dark, but we have tiki torches around the campsite, probably to ward off bobcats and bears - which I'm trying not to think about.

"Having fun yet?" he asks with a chuckle.

"Actually, it's not too bad. I met a few of the families. Had a good hotdog. Made a s'more that rocked my world."

"That must've been a really good s'more."

"Harper told me she's going to bunk with Olivia's family."

"And you?"

"No room at the inn for me just yet. I might just sleep in my car," I suggest.

"Um, no. You can't sleep in your car, Indy."

"There are locks on my doors…"

"You'll sleep with me."

I swallow hard. "Excuse me?"

"I'm in a big tent alone. There's plenty of room."

I don't think I've ever felt so uncomfortable. "Kent, I can't do that."

"Indy, I'm not going to maul you. I promise."

"I didn't say that."

"Look," he says, turning slightly to face me. "I'm not going to lie. I would love to date you. I made a horrible mistake letting you go in high school. But I know you're not interested. I get it. I know you have feelings for Dawson."

I cough. "I don't have feelings…"

"Please don't try to deny it. You might get struck by lightning, and I'm sitting right next to you."

I smile. "You're a great guy, Kent."

"But you're not attracted to me like that. Right?"

I bite both of my lips. "I'm sorry."

"Me too. But we can still be friends, right?" Gosh, that question makes me think of my current predicament with Dawson. It's been several days since I saw him standing in the doorway of my office, and I miss him more than I care to admit.

"Of course."

"Okay. Good. So as your friend, please sleep in my tent. I can't be worried about you up in your car. And I know you don't want to leave Harper alone down here."

I sigh. "You make a good case."

"I thought about being a lawyer."

"But you settled on PE teacher?" I ask with a laugh.

"Better clientele."

"Fine. I'll sleep in your tent." I finish my hot chocolate and place the cup on the ground by my feet.

"I was sorry to hear about Dawson's mother," he says offhandedly.

"What did you just say?"

"Wait. You didn't know?"

"Know what?"

"She's on her death bed, from what I heard. Dawson went to say his goodbyes."

My heart squeezes, and I have to fight back tears. I was so rude to him before he left, and now he thinks I'm shacking up with Kent while he grieves.

For a moment, I consider leaving and trying to find him. But he's not even in the state, and I can't do that to Harper. My cell phone has virtually no signal out here, so I can't even text him. I feel helpless.

"He didn't tell me," I say softly.

"He didn't tell you? But you guys are so close." Kent seems genuinely surprised.

"We had a little… argument…"

"Oh. Well, try not to let it bother you so you can enjoy this experience with Harper. I shouldn't have said anything. I really thought you knew."

"No, it's okay," I say, trying to sound unaffected. "I'm sure he'll reach out to me when he gets back."

We chat for awhile longer before everyone turns in. I make sure Harper goes into her tent before sneaking into Kent's. He was right - it is a large tent, plenty big enough for at least four people. We place our bags between us before I slip into my sleeping bag.

All I can think about is Dawson. Where is he right now? Is he standing vigil beside his mother's bed? How is he saying goodbye to the woman who made his life miserable for so many years? And does he think I don't care?

I stare at the roof of the tent until I finally pass out from exhaustion.

THE NEXT MORNING, we have a big breakfast together with sausage, bacon and eggs before everyone treks out on their own. Some people are hiking while others are fishing in the small lake about a quarter of a mile from our campsite.

Harper asked to go on a scavenger hunt with a group of kids who were being chaperoned by one of the girl's teenage brothers. He's an Eagle Scout, so I feel comfortable letting him guide the group.

"What are you doing?" Kent asks when he sees me sitting on a rock down by the creek.

"Pondering."

"Mind if I sit?"

I pat the rock next to me and smile.

"So what are you pondering, Indy? The meaning of life? Your purpose here on Earth?" he asks dramatically.

"I'm pondering why Sissy Davenport came on this camping trip wearing a full face of clown makeup and her skinny jeans." Sissy is a teacher at the school, but she's more known for her vanity than her teaching skills.

Kent lets out a loud laugh that echoes through the forest. "Well, I wasn't expecting that response."

I chuckle. "I probably shouldn't have said that, but come on. I doubt she's going to catch a husband way out here unless he's a fugitive on the run or something."

"You're funny, Indy Stone." He skips a rock across the pond, a talent that has always impressed me. I've never been able to do it correctly.

"Miss Stone!" someone calls from behind me. Whoever it is, they're panicked about something.

161

I stand up and turn to see the teenage boy who was leading the scavenger hunt - I think his name is Samuel - standing at the edge of the creek bed.

"What's wrong, Samuel?" Kent says before I can speak.

"It's Harper. She's... she's missing!"

~

THERE ARE few things in life that will bring you straight to your knees than hearing the words that your child is missing. My brain feels like lightning is zipping around, bouncing from one side of my skull to the other. I feel Kent's arm around my waist, stabilizing me from fainting and falling straight into the creek.

"It's going to be okay, Indy. We'll find her. I promise," I hear him saying. His voice is soothing, but obviously full of fear.

In the last hour, we've managed to mobilize our group to start a search party. The owner of the campground has also called in additional searchers.

All I can hear is the sound of people calling Harper's name. I honestly don't know how she could've gotten so far out of earshot, and that terrifies me. Maybe she can't hear us for some other reason.

"I was able to get in touch with the local news channel, and they're running emergency alerts right now. Also the radio station..." I hear one man saying. I don't even know his name, but I feel gratitude that he's trying to find Harper.

I stand there by the extinguished campfire having no idea what to do. Kent told me we should stay here in case Harper finds her way back. But I want to do something. I just don't know what.

"Has anyone checked my car?" I ask, knowing that it's a stupid question.

"Yes," Kent says, rubbing my arm. "We'll find her..."

He keeps saying that. I hope he's right. I think he just doesn't know what else to say.

"I don't understand how this happened."

"Samuel said they got bored doing the scavenger hunt after awhile, so the kids decided to play hide and seek. Harper took off up one of the hills, but no one could find her. After half an hour, he came back to tell us."

"But how did she get so far away?" I say out loud to no one in particular.

"We don't know, Indy," Kent says softly.

"Unless she's hurt. God, what if she's hurt?" I ask, staring up into Kent's eyes. He looks worried. "What if she fell down a mountain or into a ravine? Or bears? Aren't there bears around here? Can we call some kind of forest ranger?"

"Indy, the rangers are already here looking with our search party. Everyone is doing all they can. We just have to wait..."

"I don't want to wait!" I yell. "I need to *do* something! That's my kid out there, for goodness sakes!"

I pace back and forth, desperate for this moment to be over. I just want to see Harper walking toward me, her bright red hair glistening under the streams of sunlight poking through to the darkened forest floor.

Hours pass as I alternate between pacing quietly and ranting and raving at Kent for no real reason. I cry. I beg. I pray. Morning turns to afternoon, and there's still no sign of her.

"The area is very heavy with vegetation," one of the experienced hikers says as he comes to give me an update. "We've covered the whole western side of the mountain all the way down into the valley. I don't know how she could've gone any further than that."

"And what about the east side?" I ask, frustrated and exhausted.

"It's very treacherous over there, and nobody here has the hiking equipment to get down there very far. I doubt that…"

"Doubt that what?"

He looks at Kent and then looks at his feet.

"Don't treat me like I'm some kind of weak woman!"

"I doubt that anyone without serious hiking skills could survive the east side, ma'am. I'm sorry to be so blunt but…"

I sit down on a log slowly, the weight of what he's just said sinking in. "God, I can't lose her. I just can't."

The hiker walks off into the woods again, and Kent joins me on the ground, his arm wrapped tightly around me. I put my head on his shoulder and sob. I can't hold it together any longer.

Kent pulls me in tighter and rocks me gently back and forth. It feels good to be held, but I wish it was Dawson. And that makes me mad at myself.

"Indy?"

I turn around and think I'm hallucinating. Dawson is standing there, a look of concern on his face.

"Dawson?" I say, standing up. Kent stands behind me. "I thought you were out of town?"

"I came back this morning. I heard the news… I came as soon as I could…"

I don't think about it. I immediately rush toward his waiting arms. He pulls me in close, and I rest my tear-stained cheek against his chest. Right now, I don't care what kind of mixed signals I'm sending. I need him like the air I breathe.

He presses his mouth against the top of my head and then against my ear. "I'm going to find Harper. I promise you. I won't rest until I do."

I pull back and look at him. His eyes are filled with tears, but he swallows hard and they retreat before they can spill over.

"They said the west side has been covered, and the east side would be almost impossible for an inexperienced hiker, much less a kid…"

He grabs my shoulders and leans down, looking me in the eyes. "When we were kids, you saved me, Indy," he says softly where only I can hear. "And now I'm going to return that favor."

He kisses my cheek softly and then heads straight for the woods before I can say another word.

CHAPTER 13

*I*t's getting dark. All of the searchers have returned, except for Dawson. There has been no sign of Harper, even after the helicopter started looking around three o'clock. When the sun started setting, the helicopter had to retreat for the night.

I'm feeling more hopeless by the minute, and now I'm worried about Dawson too.

"You need to eat something, Indy," Kent urges yet again, holding out a hotdog on a skewer. I brush it away.

"I told you I'm not hungry."

I stare into the dark woods, hoping to see any sign of Dawson or Harper. But there's no light. There's just nothing. And it's getting colder. I don't think she can survive the night.

With every passing hour, the reality sets in more and more. I've prayed to God. To Jesus. To Danny. To my dead grandmother.

"Where is he?" I say out loud. Kent sighs.

"I'm sure Dawson is fine."

"You don't even like Dawson," I say flatly.

"Sure I do. I just kind of wish you didn't." His attempt at humor isn't landing well at all. "Sorry. Wrong time. Just trying to break the tension a bit."

I sit down beside him and stare at the fire. "You know what's weird?"

"What?"

I take the hot dog from his hands and pinch off a piece. I have no appetite, but falling out from low blood sugar wouldn't help Harper and would divert resources from the search for her.

"My whole world used to be clients back in Charleston. And now my whole world is out there lost in the woods."

"I don't think you just mean Harper."

"What makes you say that?"

"I saw how you looked at him, Indy. How you ran to him like he was your lifeline. You love Dawson."

"Now isn't the time for this…"

"No. You're right. But when this is all over… when he brings your daughter out of those woods safe and sound… you need to remember this conversation."

I hear his words, but I'm stuck on "safe and sound". Is that even possible?

I FEEL like I'm losing my mind. As I watch the sun rise through the small spaces between the trees, I feel hopeless. Dawson never came back. Harper hasn't come back. My world is imploding around me, and there's not a damn thing I can do about it.

The search team has tripled in size, and they're about to go out again. I overheard some official-looking guy saying that this was about to turn into a recovery mission instead of a rescue because of the low nighttime temperatures.

I feel like I've cried all of the tears I have. I want to cry more, but there's nothing there. Kent keeps force feeding me water and hot dogs. I swear I never want to see another hot dog again for the rest of my life.

"I'm going stir crazy here," I say to Kent. He hasn't left my side since this whole thing began. He's a good friend. No one else really talks to me now. I think they don't know what to say. I've bitten off a few heads that said the "wrong" thing to me, so most people keep their distance. A part of me wonders how I could have so much training as a therapist and not be able to deal with this crisis better than I am right now.

"I know. I'm so sorry this is happening to you, Indy. You don't deserve it." He puts his arm my shoulder for the thousandth time and I lay my head down.

"Maybe I do deserve it," I say softly.

"No. You don't. Stop saying that."

I sit up and stick my hands out to warm them by the fire. "I've made some mistakes in my life, Kent."

"We all have."

"It's only recently that I started to think this was it, you know? I finally had my life together. I finally felt like the pieces were sliding together in my favor."

"Don't give up hope, Indy. She's out there. They both are."

I stand up and move closer to the fire, watching it flicker in the last pieces of darkness shadowing our campsite. "She's my daughter. She's not just my niece anymore. She's not just some stranger that had to come live with me. She's my world, Kent. I didn't tell her that. She doesn't know how much I love her right now."

He stands and puts his hands on my shoulders. "Yes, she does."

"Indy?" a woman says from behind me. Her voice is frantic.

"Yes?"

"We've got to go. The searchers think they've found something a few miles down the east side, at the lowest part of the river. We'll have to drive there."

Oh God. The river. It dawns on me that I have no idea if she even knows how to swim. How can a mother not know that about her child?

"Is it Harper? Is she alive?" I ask as I follow her up the trail to the parking lot.

"I don't know," she calls back to me. "That's all they would tell me. That they found 'something'." I push back the fear that "something" is her body.

Kent runs along beside me, and we jump in his truck. I'm in no shape to drive. The drive to the river is steep, and we finally have to get out at a trailhead for experienced hikers. Getting down to the area we need to go is challenging to say the least. The drive alone was several miles, but the hike is grueling and almost completely vertical.

I slide the remainder of the way on a pile of dead leaves and almost run into a tree before getting to my feet again. The woman, a local hiker herself, leads us by using some navigational tool she has in her hand.

"Anybody here?" she calls, which makes me worry she's lost just as much as we are.

In the distance, I hear voices that create a low rumble across the forest floor. "Over here!" a male voice yells out.

We all jog in that direction, and I can't ever recall my heart beating so hard in my chest. It truly feels like some kind of alien is trying to escape from the center of my body.

We run through some thick brush, and I can hear the roar of the river as we approach it. I trip, but Kent catches me just in time before I face plant and cause myself injuries yet again. I'm still so sore from my accident, but right now my body is running on pure adrenaline.

"What did you…" I start to ask, but before I can finish my sentence, I see her. Harper is standing by the river with a thick fleece blanket wrapped around her. She's standing. She's breathing. She looks exhausted, and her hair is tangled and wild from obviously being wet at some point. But she is alive. "Harper!"

She turns and sees me, and tears immediately spring from her eyes as she runs toward me, dropping the blanket along the way. As she barrels into me, the force almost knocks me over. I feel Kent prop me up once again from behind.

Her face is buried in my chest, and she's sobbing. I can't understand all that she's saying except for occasional fragments of sentences.

"I'm so sorry…"

"I was so scared…"

"I thought I'd never see you again…"

"Mommy…"

I kneel down and put my hands on her cheeks. "Are you okay, sweetie? We were so worried about you. I prayed and prayed you were okay…"

"I'm okay. It was so cold last night…"

"I know. Oh my God, I'm just so thankful you're okay," I say, hugging her tightly again. The searchers surround us, smiles on every face. I stand up and look at each of them. "I cannot thank you all enough for your tireless dedication to bringing my daughter home. Who can I thank for finding Harper?"

I look around the circle of people, but then they break apart and everyone looks toward the river. Standing there, with the first rays of sunlight behind him like some kind of superhero angel, is Dawson.

He bites his lips and cocks his head to the side. "Dawson found you?" I ask Harper without taking my eyes off of him.

"Yes. He found me last night and kept me warm. That's

where I got this blanket," she says, picking it back up off the ground and wrapping it around herself.

"Come on, Harper. Let's get you back to camp so you can have something to eat, okay?" Kent says, aware that I need a moment with Dawson alone. She looks at me, obviously worried about splitting up again.

"It's okay, honey. Dawson and I will be up in just a second, okay? Don't drive off without us," I say to Kent with a wink. Harper hugs me again before heading up the steep incline with the rest of the searchers.

Dawson walks toward me, and I close the distance between us. I hug him tightly and bury my head in his chest, tears finally reappearing.

"I can never thank you enough," is all I manage the eke out.

"I love Harper," he says softly. "I would've never stopped looking for her."

"What happened? How did she get here?"

"Let's get out of here. I'll tell you the whole story later, okay?"

"Your mom... Kent told me she was sick... I had no idea, Dawson. I'm so sorry I wasn't nicer to you..."

"My mom passed away right before I flew back."

"Oh God, Dawson. I... don't know what to say..."

He puts his hands on my cheeks and kisses my forehead for a long moment. "I'm exhausted and running on fumes right now, but I have a lot I need to say to you. Let's go home, okay?"

I nod, and we walk arm in arm back to the truck.

EVERYONE HAS GONE home except for Kent, Dawson, Harper and me. The campfire is dying down, but we were all too tired - physically and emotionally - to start the drive home just yet.

"I'm so sorry I wandered off," Harper says again. "We were playing hide and seek, and I heard the river. I thought it was close, but then I fell down a long hill. I guess I was going the wrong direction beside the river."

"And I think she just couldn't hear the searchers calling her name," Dawson says, taking a sip of his hot chocolate. "That river is really loud."

"So how did you find her?" Kent asks as he starts tamping out the fire.

"Well, no one had checked the east side, so I knew to go there. And kids are more likely to follow the noise, thinking it might lead them back to civilization. So I just started walking along the river, yelling for Harper. By the time I found her, it was late last night and we couldn't get back. My cell wouldn't give me a signal, so we just cuddled up last night and hoped we wouldn't freeze to death."

"How did you have a blanket?" I ask.

"I guess you didn't notice I left here with a backpack full of supplies last night?" he asks, a sly smile on his face.

"I was a little preoccupied," I say with a laugh.

"Am I in trouble?" Harper finally asks.

I pull her close and rest my head on top of hers. "No, but don't you ever do that to me again, okay?"

"I won't. I promise."

"You're all I have in this world, Harper Stone."

"Hey!" both men say at the same time.

"And you guys. You are both very important cogs in the Indy Stone wheel."

"That has to be the worst joke you've ever made," Dawson says with a laugh. "Ladies, I think it's time we go home."

"I agree one-hundred percent," I say as I stand up. We've

already packed the vehicles with most of our gear, or at least the other campers did for us.

I'm so tired, and the long drive ahead of me isn't appealing, but since we have three vehicles I don't have a choice. I cannot wait to get home, but first I have one more thing to do.

"Can you guys head up without me? I need to chat with Kent for a moment."

Dawson nods and holds Harper's hand as they head up the trail.

"Listen, Kent, I just want to say how incredible you were throughout this whole thing. I couldn't have survived this without your strength, so thank you. Really. From the bottom of my heart." I hug him tightly. I really did underestimate him as a person.

"You're welcome, Indy. But the man you really need to thank is standing up there beside your car."

"I know. What he did was amazing."

"Can I say something?"

"Of course," I say as we start walking toward the trail.

"That man worships the ground you walk on, Indy. He may not be perfect, but I think he might be worth the effort."

"You're one smart man, Kent Akers," I say, sliding my arm through his.

I LEAN my head back against the patio chair and sigh. I've never felt so exhausted in my life. Every muscle aches, but that's to be expected. It's just that I didn't know that my mind and heart would literally feel bruised and achy too. I'm "wrung out" as my grandmother used to say.

"Here you go," Dawson says when he joins me on the patio with a cup of coffee.

"She still asleep?" I ask, suddenly worried that Harper might disappear from her bed or something. She's been out like a light for hours now, and it's only nine o'clock at night.

"Yep. She's snoring like a freight train." He laughs as he takes a seat across from me and warms his hands on his mug.

"If you're cold, we can go inside…" I suggest.

"No," he says. "This is nothing compared to last night."

There's a quiet moment between us before I speak. "Dawson, you're my hero. You know that, right?"

He smiles. "Well, you've always been my hero, Indy Stone."

I take a sip of my coffee, trying to hide my smile. "Seriously, Harper wouldn't have survived the night without you. If you hadn't come…"

"Don't say that. I did come. And she's snug in her bed as we speak."

"I know but…"

"Let's not talk about what ifs. Okay?" I can tell it's making him anxious to think about what would've happened. "Do you have any tattoos?" What a random question.

"Um… No… Why?"

"I'm one of those rare military guys who really doesn't like tattoos all that much. But I have one. Want to see it?"

"Okay…" I have no idea how we got on this subject. He stands up and lifts his sweatshirt to reveal a small tattoo on his right pec muscle. I heat up a bit when I see his muscles on full display. I want to reach out and touch his defined abs but think better of it. "What does it say?"

"It's the number '587'," he says and then sits down like I should know what that means.

"Was that like your solider ID number or something?"

"No." He takes a sip of his coffee.

"Your locker combination?"

"Not even close."

"Okay, I give up. What does '587' mean?"

"May 1987."

"What happened in... Wait. Wasn't that when we met?"

He chuckles. "There you go..."

"You tattooed the date we met? But why?"

"Because I never wanted to forget you, Indy."

My emotions are raw, and I feel my eyes swelling with tears again. I swear a car insurance commercial might make me cry right now.

"I don't know what to say."

"I told my mother about you."

"What?"

"When I went to see her. She had one lucid day, almost like she was waiting for me. I was able to really talk to her, Indy."

"I'm so happy for you, Dawson."

"I told her how her marriages and all those men affected me as a kid. And as an adult. I said things I'd never said before, and she just listened. She didn't argue or defend herself. She just said she was sorry. She had never said that before. And she told me she loved me. I can't remember ever hearing that before."

"Wow."

"And I met her husband. Crazily enough, he seems to be a good guy. He loved her. Grieved the next day when she passed." He chokes up a bit and then continues. "I told her that you were back in Peach Valley, and that I love you."

"Dawson..."

"Please let me finish."

"Okay."

"My mother made so many mistakes in her life. More than anyone I know. But in the end, she found love. She kept trying to fill some void in herself, but she was happy when she died. I can't help but wonder how happy she would've been if she'd just settled and not taken that chance."

I sit quietly, letting him talk.

"When I showed up at the campsite, my PTSD was in full effect. I was shaking inside. My heart was pounding. I could barely hear you speak over the pounding in my ears. I felt ill equipped to find Harper. But the moment I saw your face and how you were depending on me... that all went away. You were my hero as a kid, and I wanted to be yours. And God, when I found her... when I saw her sitting by the river, shivering... my heart broke. I don't see her as your niece or even your daughter. I see her as *my* daughter."

"Dawson, what are you saying?"

He stands up and pulls me up with him, his hand on my cheek. "I'm saying that you and Harper are my family, and I want to be with you."

"You're with us everyday."

"No, I mean forever, Indy."

"What?"

"I'm not scared anymore."

"Scared?"

"Of forever. Of marriage."

"Oh..." I feel so confused. "So this means..."

He smiles and kisses my lips softly before looking at me again. "It means that I want to spend all of my future days with you and Harper. And when I take my last breath, it's your face I want to see. There is nobody else for me, Indy."

He pulls me close and presses his lips against my forehead. "Will you please do me the honor of dating me for a proper amount of time until I can get down on one knee and give you a modest rock that fits my teacher's salary?"

I laugh so hard that I fear I'll wake Harper up.

"That is... if you love me too?" he says, pulling back and looking at me.

I go stone faced for a moment, just to mess with him, and then a smile spreads across my face. "I love you too, Dawson Woods."

He pulls me close again and we stand there for the longest time. I finally give in to the flood of emotions that are bubbling inside of me. Relief. Joy. Love. And Dawson holds me there as my body jolts from the tears that release like a broken dam.

EPILOGUE

*S*ix *Months Later...*
   May in Peach Valley is as beautiful as I remember. The pollen passed early this year, and I'm ever so thankful for allergy medicine. I've been able to keep my sneezing fits to a minimum.

I stand in front of the floor length mirror and stare at myself. This is a place I never expected to be. In a small country church with creaky hardwood floors and gorgeous stained glass windows.

"Mommy, you look like a fairy princess!" Harper says when she enters the room.

"And you look like a queen!" I say back as I marvel at how grown up she looks in her pink bridesmaid dress. Danny would be so proud. I can feel his presence today.

"Is Dawson out there?"

"Well, he didn't run away!" Harper has a keen sense of humor.

"I guess that's a good thing, huh?"

When he proposed on Valentine's Day, I really hadn't expected it. Over the last six months, we've forged a bond that will never be broken. Honestly, it no longer mattered to me whether we had that piece of paper, but it started mattering more to him.

"Look at you. My beautiful baby sister," Amy says as she enters the bridal room. She runs her fingers along the edge of my veil. "Mom would be so proud of you, Indy."

I hug her tightly and quietly thank God for a second chance at having a sister. Our friendship has truly grown these last few months, and Harper has benefited so much from having new cousins who have become her best friends.

"Group hug?" Tabitha, being her normal boisterous self, comes barging into the room with a big grin on her face. She pulls me, Harper and Amy into a hug. "It's almost time, girls."

"I know. I'm a nervous wreck. It might be a second marriage, but it's my first wedding." My hands are shaking as I put on my earrings.

"No need to be nervous. You're getting the fairytale ending every girl dreams of," Amy says, taking over and helping me get my earrings on.

"I'm blessed, that's for sure," I say, looking at Harper. I'm amazed at the whirlwind of a life I've led during the last year. Losing a brother, gaining a daughter, reconnecting with the love of my life.

It hasn't always been easy, but it's been worth it. There are no doubts about that.

"Knock knock!" I hear Dawson say from around the corner.

"Don't you come in here!" Tabitha yells back. "It's bad luck to see the bride before the wedding!"

"I'm not coming in!" Dawson says with a laugh. "But we can talk around this corner, right?"

I shrug my shoulders. "I guess that doesn't break the rules," I call back.

"Ah, there's the voice of my bride to be. Hey, sweetie…"

179

"Gag!" Harper says with a giggle as all three of them leave the room.

Dawson sticks his hand through the crack in the door, and I walk over and take it in mine.

"Are you nervous?" I ask him, wondering if any lingering doubts about marriage are bothering him.

"Not a bit. I'm marrying my best friend today."

My heart melts. "No cold feet?"

"Nope. My feet are as warm as my heart."

I laugh. "Have you been working on that joke?"

"A little," he says before walking around the corner unexpectedly.

"Dawson! You can't…"

I look up and realize he has his neck tie tied around his eyes. "I promise I can't see a thing, but I can't go a moment longer without doing this…"

He pulls me into an embrace as he presses his lips against mine. That just never gets old.

"Hmmmm. I think we might want to keep that tie handy on the honeymoon," I say teasingly.

"Okay, you need to stop saying things like that or I might not be able to concentrate on what the minister is saying."

"Hey, love birds, it's about time," Kent says from the hallway. He's Dawson's best man, which is something I never thought I'd see in my lifetime. After Harper's rescue, the two men became fast friends when Dawson realized how much Kent helped me.

"Well, I guess I'll see you at the front of the church in a few minutes," Dawson says before kissing me one more time.

"See you there," I say back.

"You look beautiful, Indy!" Kent calls as they start walking up the hallway.

"Thanks!"

"If things don't work out with this guy, I'm always available!" Kent says with a laugh. I see Dawson punch him in the arm.

"Hey, that's not funny..." Dawson says as they turn the corner.

As I stand there in my final quiet moment before entering the church, I think about all of the blessings I've had over the last few months and my eyes well with tears.

Things didn't start out like I wanted as a kid. Life was tough, in fact. But I've realized that it's only in times of darkness that we can actually see the light. We don't appreciate the light when it's all we see, but we sure appreciate it when we've been stuck in the darkness for too long.

"Ready?" Harper asks from the doorway. She's walking me down the aisle.

"Absolutely," I say, taking her hand in mine as we head toward the door leading into the sanctuary.

"Do you think I should call Dawson daddy?" she asks.

"I think you should call Dawson whatever you want."

"I think I'd like to call him Pop," she says softly.

"He'll love that," I reply. "And so would your Daddy." Harper smiles as she opens the door and we both walk toward a very bright, new future.

WANT to read more books by Rachel Hanna? Head over to Amazon to read these other great books!

THE JANUARY COVE SERIES:
The One For Me
Loving Tessa
Falling For You
Finding Love

All I Need
Secrets And Soulmates
Sweet Love
Choices of the Heart
Faith, Hope & Love
Spying On The Billionaire
Second Chance Christmas

THE WHISKEY RIDGE Series
Starting Over
Taking Chances
Home Again
Always A Bridesmaid
The Billionaire's Retreat